APHRA BEHN – Dispa

Ross Laidlaw was born in Aberdeen in 1931, growing up in Edinburgh and the Borders. He has pursued an unusual and varied career, from National Service in Hong Kong, through Cambridge University and on to Africa, where his adventures led him through teaching in Kenya, co-managing a farm, hunting trips in the Kalahari, and painting buffalo murals in a Bulawayo bar, before returning to Britain in 1958. After working as a door to door salesman, factory hand and more, he taught in England, Canada and Wales, and in Edinburgh. He 'broke out' of teaching to eventually become an assistant archivist at Durham Record Office – via a diploma from the University of Wales – but returned to teaching at Dunbar in Scotland.

Ross Laidlaw has at least one literary antecedent, Willie Laidlaw, poet and secretary to Walter Scott. He himself has also two previous publications, *The Lion is Rampant* (Molendinar, 1979), and *The Linton Porcupine* (Canongate, 1984). He lives in East Lothian, where his interests include hill-walking, and baroque music, to politics, S.N.P., and archery.

APHRA BEHN –
Dispatch'd from Athole

The Journal of Aphra Behn's Secret Mission to Scotland, in 1689

Ross Laidlaw

BALNAIN

Printed and bound in Britain by BPCC Wheatons, Exeter
Design by Sarah Fraser

The publisher gratefully acknowledges subsidy from the Scottish Arts Council towards the publication of this volume.

Acknowledgements:
The Map of Scotland by Herman Moll, 1714, (and details) are reproduced by kind permission of the Trustees of the National Library of Scotland.

Published in 1992 by
Balnain Books
Druim House,
LochLoy Road,
Nairn IV12 5LF

British Library Cataloguing in Publication Data
A catalogue record for this book is available from the British Library

ISBN 0-872557-17-1

Dedication:

To Marjorie and Douglas Mickel,
and to John and Effie Allardyce,
for all their kindness

CONTENTS

The NORTH PART of
GREAT BRITAIN
Called
SCOTLAND.
By Herman Moll Geographer 1714
To the Right Honourable
IOHN Earl of MARR
One of Her Majesty's PRINCIPAL
SECRETARIES of STATE
This MAP
THE NORTH
OR
BRITISH
SEA
PENTLAND FIRTH
ORKNEY ISL.
Dungsby Head
Faro Head
The Ord Head
FIRTH OF DORNOCH
FIRTH OF CROMARTIE
FIRTH OF MURRAY
FIRTH OF FORTH
St Ebbsheads
Holy I
Farne I
Cocket I
P. of SOUTH
BRITAIN
CUMBERLAND
Called
ENGLAND
DURHAM
Carlisle
Durham
Newcastle
Solway Firth
THE IRISH SEA
THE FIRTH OF CLYD
The Mul of Cantire
The Mul of Galloway
Belfast
Carick Fergus
Glenarm Bay
Colerasne
Rachlin I
Loch Tarbat
Tiree or Ile
Col I
Rum I
Sea Crest
Loch Eriboll
ISLANDS
MULL
GALLOWAY
ANANDALE
NITHISDALE
TIVIOTDALE
ANGUS
MERNS
BAMFF
STRATH NAVER
XXVIII
XXIV
XX
XII
VIII
IV
0

TRANSCRIBER'S NOTE

At the beginning of December 1988, I was asked by the head of an old-established East Lothian family if I would have a look at a bundle of papers which he'd found among family archives. He thought that they might be of historical interest, and knowing that I had formerly been an archivist, wondered if I might be willing to transcribe them. The bundle arrived shortly afterwards – about two hundred leaves of manuscript in a late 17th century hand, written I thought by the same person.

I skimmed through the first few pages, and it looked as if the manuscript consisted of a series of draft letters (interleaved among pages of a personal journal), from Aphra Behn to one Gilbert Burnet, concerning plans of John Graham of Claverhouse to help King James II to regain his throne.

'Aphra who?' would I suspect be the reaction of most people, and I admit that I had then scarcely heard of the lady myself; about Gilbert Burnet I was totally ignorant. Claverhouse, as everyone knows, is 'Bonnie Dundee' who was killed at Killiecrankie in his moment of victory, in 1689. An afternoon's digging in the Central and National Libraries in Edinburgh uncovered enough basic biographical details to put me in the picture re. Aphra Behn and Burnet. (See Appendix.)

Aphra Behn emerged as a fascinating and complex personality – spy, poet, novelist and playwright, passionate lover (of both sexes it would seem!), political activist, thinker (she subscribed to the Atomic Theory and Determinism), an early champion of Racial and Sex Equality. Gilbert Burnet came over as a kind of British Cardinal Richelieu-cum-Voltaire, a clergyman who seems to have known and influenced just about everyone of consequence (political and cultural) of his time. An arch 'fixer', he seems to have virtually masterminded the public relations side of the Glorious Revolution.

In view of her early track record, I couldn't help wondering if Aphra Behn was acting as a spy, with Burnet as her 'control'. However, a little further investigation disclosed that Dundee's campaign in support of James II began only after William and Mary had been proclaimed King and Queen in Edinburgh. That was on April 11th 1689 – ***five days before Aphra Behn's death!***

An intriguing anomaly! – unless of course the manuscript were to reveal that Aphra Behn or Burnet had prior knowledge of Dundee's intentions. What the manuscript, in the course of transcription, did reveal, was a body of startling and hitherto completely unknown facts – which sheds fresh light on certain events that took place in 1689, and calls for a degree of re-appraisal concerning them.

P.S. – For the convenience of the modern reader, I have broken up Aphra Behn's journal into two Parts, according to location, and given the entries 'Chapter Headings' suggested by appropriate words in the text. Wherever continuity between one entry and the next is not readily apparent, I have taken the liberty of inserting a short connecting passage of my own. The drafts of letters to Gilbert Burnet and Andrew Fletcher, 'dispatch'd from Athole' and other places on her Itinerary, I have not included in the transcription for two reasons. Firstly, they are in essence condensations of certain passages in the Journal, so to reproduce them would be merely repeating information. Secondly, they are written partly in some kind of code; one can get the gist of these encoded sections by comparing them with the relevant passages in the Journal, but exact transcription isn't possible – for this transcriber at least!

In case anyone should wish to know a little more about some of the people, places and events mentioned in the Journal, I have added supplementary information at the end, under 'Notes' and 'Appendix'. I should perhaps point out that these are the results of ***ad hoc*** 'instant' research undertaken at odd moments in the course of transcribing the Journal, rather than of any prior knowledge; I can only hope that the haste with which they were compiled is not too glaringly apparent!

Aphra Behn dates the entries in her Journal prior to April 1689 thus: 1688/9. From the late 12th century Lady Day, 25th March, was generally accepted in England as the opening of the year, and continued so, officially, till 1752, when 1st January was adopted instead. However, by the late 17th century, the Continental usage of dating the New Year from January 1st had become widely accepted in England and it was quite fashionable to date documents (as Pepys does) written between 1st January and 25th March, according to both systems.

R.L.

PART ONE

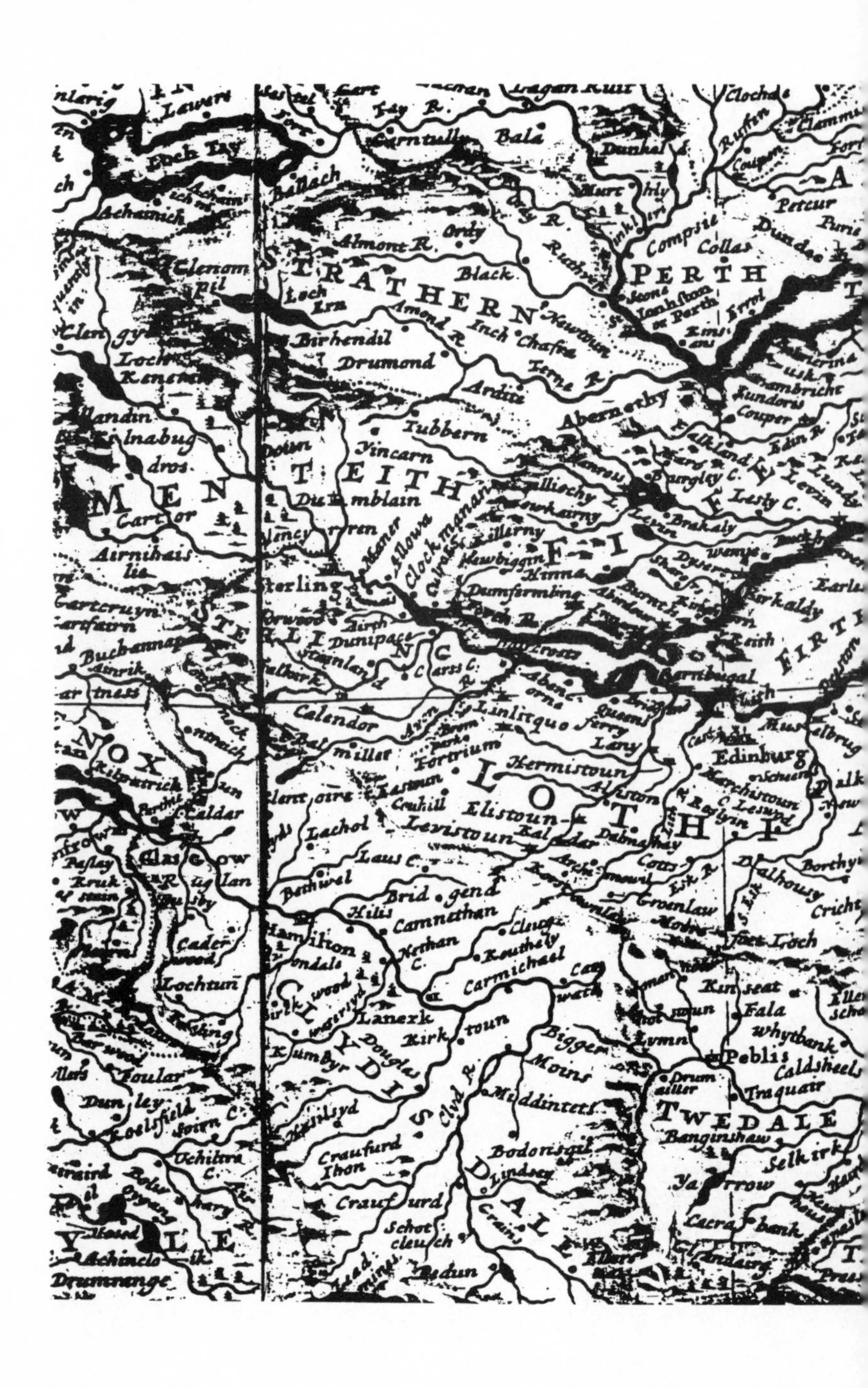

Loch Tay
Bala
Fay R.
Almont R.
Ordy
Black
STRATHERN
PERTH
Collas
Compsie
Dundee
Newtoun
Inch
Chafre
Birhendil
Drumond
Arditte
Tubbern
Abernethy
Yincarn
TEITH
Dumblain
MEN
Falkland
Lesly C.
Clockmanan
Allowa
Stirling
Dunipace
FIFE
Kirkaldy
Burntisland
Calendor
Linlitquo
Edinburg
Hermistoun
Levistoun
Elistoun
LOTHI
Glasgow
Bothwel
Brid gend
Hamilton
Carmichael
Lanerk
Kirk toun
Douglas
Biggar
Peblis
Traquair
TWEDALE
Selkirk
Yarrow
Craufurd
Schot cleuch
Foular
Kilpatrick
Calder
Paslay
Lochtun
Achincloik
Drumnenge
Middintees
Bodonisgil
Lindsay
DALE

LOTHIANE

Brechin
Dun
Montrose
Kynard
Red Cast.
Kelly
Ethie
FIRTH
St. Andrews
Balcomy
Fyfe Ness
Careill
East & W. Anstruther
May I.
Pettenweem
Monans
OF FORTH
The Bass
North Berwick
Tallon Cast
Tyne R.
Dunbar
Tynningham
St. Ebbeshead
Coldingham
Byres
Haddington
Saltoun
Dunglas Castle
Aitoun
Coppersmith
Aimouth
Yester
Ormestoun
Barwick Uppon Tweed
Duns
Grinla
Coldstr
MERS
Snenk
Twesel
Holy I.
Lauder
Hirsel
Gordoun
Tweed
Learmouth
Thirlstaine
Kelso
NORTHUM
Belford
Farne I.
Wuller
Clefford
Nisbot
Hyndhoope
Alnewick
Cocket
Iedburg
Black chester
Coket R.
Felton
IOTDALE
Edderstein
Ellsedon
Lyne
B R

1.
‘ A HARD TEST ’

London,
March 4th, 1688/9.

IN THE NAME OF GOD AMEN: ’tis fitting you’ll allow (and you but read in this History a little space) I should choose to preface this my Journall begun the fourth day of March in the year of God 1689, in the Manner and Forme of a Last Will and Testament, rather than with an Epistle Dedicatory as is the custom.

For I, Aphra Behn of London in the County of Middlesex, relict and gentlewoman, being sick in bodie tho’ sound in mind, having but little of Worldly Goods to give, do bequeath unto such of my friends (in especiall to you, most ador’d Mazarine) as may chance to read herein, this little Work the last shall be writ by Astrea’s pen. And if you deem the matters I shall relate so fantastickal they must needs be feign’d (especially as being recounted by one of the female sex), then a pox on it, the Woman damns the Poet, (as I've said in another place).

But to my tale; yesterday came Honest Hoyle of the Inner Temple to my lodgings here in Dorset Street bearing a Letter from Doctor Gilbert Burnet, he requesting verie civille that I permit the Doctor to visit me at my convenience. Had other than Hoyle been the bearer I'd have bid him begone, saying to tell the Doctor I'd not see him – for you should know I owe the Doctor small goodwill, he having censur'd some of my Plays and Verse as being Licentious (tho' and a man had writ 'em, 'twere no matter). However, Hoyle pleading with such eloquence on the Doctor's behalf that I suffer him to visit me (as being a lawyer I suppose he'd acquir'd sufficiency of skills to persuade), I suffered my Resolution to be melted, more perhaps for the affection I yet bear towards Hoyle than for other cause I daresay, and gave consent.

And so today a little before twelve of the clock, arriv'd Doctor Burnet; a Scotchman, much of an age with myself (which is to say betwixt forty and fifty years), learned and quick of mind also, much travell'd especially in France and the Low Countries, countenance frank and open, of a verie inquiring and loquacious Disposition (tho' something indiscreet and censurious) but verie kindly and well-dispos'd in his Nature.

For a little space we conversed of light and trifling matters: the winter just passed that was so unseasonable hard betwixt Advent and Epiphany (tho' not so bitter cold as the Great Frost of '84 when verie Thames froze over), Robert Gould's satirick Poem just out (which the Doctor allow'd had some Wit but otherwise poor stuff full of spite and complainings against poets more gifted than himself, in which companie was numbered the modern Sappho, to wit one Aphra Behn), a new Dramatick Work by Mr. Tate about the Queen of Carthage with musick by Mr. Henry

Purcell, presently a-writing but expected to come out this year. Also he was so kind as to praise my own new Poem to Queen Mary – which civillity as soon transpir'd was but a Syren Ruse to flatter and entrap; for then he besought me I should write a Pindarick Poem celebrating the Deeds of the King.

–The Prince of Orange, I presume you mean! I burst out with some heat, –you should know better, Sir, than urge such a Request on one who knows no other King than James.

–Well well, no matter, reply'd he in a soothing manner (observing my chagreen), –I did but make triall of the waters. And do you truly love your Sovereign? Inquires he with great earnestness.

–With all my heart, I cry.

–And would act to serve his Interests, (continues he) –e'en tho' such service might seem dis-service?

–I think you speak in Riddles, Sir; but yes, if 'twere truly to serve him notwithstanding it might appear other, I believe I would so act.

–I rejoyce to hear it Madam, for I fear I must put you to a Hard Test. Mr. Kemp* as you know was permitted to cross over into France; 'twas myself prevailed in that accomodation, upon the Prince of Orange – I must name him such for I perceive you'll not suffer me to call him King. (This he says smiling to show he did but jest, and in so engaging a manner I was quite disarm'd.) –And if matters were but suffered to rest so, (continues he) –'twould be a happy Resolution of 'em. But I fear lest Mr. Kemp should take a fancy to return home, or be persuaded so to do by false counsellors.

–Speed the Day! I cry'd, –it cannot come too early.

–Such Loyaltie does you Honour, return'd the Doctor,

* alias King James VII and II - see notes

—yet consider what must follow should Mr. Kemp return; bloodie Civill War as in his Father's time, with brother's hand lifted against brother and son's against father. And to what end? He'd ne'er prevail; the people will not suffer Mr. Kemp to rule 'em twice, without he forswear Papistry if not for himself then for his Son at the least — a thing he'll never do. To essay a Homecoming and to fail in that Enterprize — which must surely happen were he to attempt it — would cause him infinitely greater hurt and Sorrow than he presently knows, and then the blood of Subjects needlessly spill'd would be perpetuall Reproach upon his Conscience, as well as furnish cause of Hatred for his Enemies.

—And how should this concern me? I inquir'd, beginning to be something troubled I knew not why.

—There is I believe but one Gentleman in all Britain, (return'd the Doctor) —who might contrive that Mr. Kemp enjoy his Own again, and that is the Lord Dundee, a Cavalier of such Spotless Honour and High Precept he'd count his Life but a feather in the balances against his Dutie to his Sovereign Liege. As I should know, (proceeded he) —for 'twas I bore to him a message from the Prince, urging Dundee that he forsake his Old Master and enter into his — the Prince's Service. Which the Lord Dundee scorn'd, inquiring did the Prince think him so base as to desert his Master in his hour of Necessitie? And is now but late return'd into Scotland. As to what he purposes to do there none can imagine, this excepting: 'tis certain he'll employ all his Rhetorick to urge the Lords of the Convention assembling at Edinburgh ten days hence, that they choose James above the Prince to reign in Scotland.

—And if he fail to move 'em? I ask.

—Oh 'tis little likely he'll succeed, reply's he; —for, saving the Earl Balcarres, Sir George MacKenzie the Lord

Advocate, and Claverhouse himself, there are like to be as many Elephants as Jacobites* in that Convention. Which may move Dundee to some desperate Venture in his Master's Cause; 'tis what I fear. Now myself and the Prince have convers'd much in this matter and have concluded as to what is best should be done. Which is this; that a Spy be sent to Edinburgh to learn of Dundee's Intentions and to discover 'em to us. And this person must needs be bold yet discreet, of a preference having some familiaritie of Spying, acquainted with the world, as well able to converse and be at ease with my Lord this or my Lady that, as to be Hail fellow, well met, with Tom, Dick or Harry. And on one head are we both perfectly agree'd; there's none by Nature and Experience** more suited to this Part, Madam, than yourself.

—You cannot think I would consent! I exclaim'd aghast. —Tho' all his friends do now forsake him and e'en his daughter Anne flaunts Orange Knacks, here's one will ne'er be traytor to her rightfull Liege King James.

Whereupon did Doctor Burnet entreat of me verie earnest and for the space of severall hours, that I be persuaded in this matter, not to be govern'd by Private Sentiment but rather by Reason'd Consideration of those things wherein Dutie ought to incline toward the Generall and Publick Good. As to which, he related many examples where Naturall Inclination was perforce suppress'd in the interest of the Common Weal, as: Abraham notwithstanding that he lov'd his Son yet made ready to sacrifice him, believing God would not have commanded it so without there had been sufficient cause, tho' 'twere hid from his understanding; and Brutus which took Caesar's life (tho'

* Burnet is paraphrasing a remark of Dundee's - see notes

** Aphra Behn had carried out a spying mission during the Dutch Wars - see Appendix.

he was Caesar's Angel as Shakespear tells) than suffer the Roman Republic to become a Tyrranie; or Nero's friend which (when the Tyrant, his fortunes being at last mis-luck'd, hearing his murtherers draw nigh would take his own life, yet at the last his courage fails him) smote the Emperor's sword-arm a buffet on the Elbow that he pierc'd his own heart and so dy'd; and many other Deeds of a like kind from Holy Writ and old Chronicles, and ended with this Remembrance, how God Himself had suffered His only Son Jesus to die on the Cross that Mankind be saved.

—Be that as it will Sir, I reply'd when he'd done, —tho' not insensible of the Logick of your Argument, I find my Heart yet opposes all your Reasonings.

—'Tis what I fear'd yet but did but expect, rejoins he, and with a Heavie Sigh takes out a packet of Papers. —I'd hoped to spare you pain, Madam, but I see 'tis not possible I should keep this Cup from you. These being dispatch'd from St. Germain were intercepted at Havre by one of our Spies. (And he gives me the Packet).

With some difficultie I untie the Ribband by which 'tis secur'd (for of a sudden my Hands are all a-tremble) and op'ning out the first Paper, find 'tis a Letter from King James at St. Germain to Richard Talbot the Earl of Tyrconnel, his Lieutenant-Generall in Ireland. Tho' not writ by his own Hand but by a Secretarie's, I knew the Letter was no Forgerie but truly from the King by the Subscription, (his Sign-Manual firstly as Duke of York, then Monarch, being verie familiar to me these eleven years from when he first became my Patron).

And as I did read, my Heart became as Lead within my Bosom, for here (and in the other Papers in the Packet — all Letters of King James to Tyrconnel, Sarsfield and other Jacobites in Ireland) were un-refutable Evidences that the Doctor's Fears were indeed well-founded, and should King James be restor'd as Sovereign then all those imagin'd Terrors which the suppos'd Discoverie of the Horrid Plot* reveal'd, would truly come to pass; Viz,

1. Promises of Moneys from France and the Pope sufficient to enable the King to rule without Parliament. Also, Troops and Munition pledg'd by the French King.
2. A Standing Armie (which is a thing abhorrent to the English Nation) to be maintain'd, its Officers to be Catholicks and its Ranks augmented by wild Irish Papists who would scruple no whit to oppress the People.
3. This to be follow'd by Generall Toleration as a means to replace Protestants by Catholicks in all the chief Offices of State — until by Force and Example Papistrie would again become the Establish'd form of Worship in England, as Tyrannie would be her form of Civill Governance.

Tho' I could not doubt that the King had been persuaded to these Policies by Base Advizers among those that shar'd his Exile — Viz, John Drummond Earl of Melfort and others of like stamp, neither could I think that these same false Counsellors would not prevail upon my poor Liege to carry through their Wicked Designs, should he be restor'd. For tho' in himself the best-intentioned and honestest of men, I will allow that the King (perchance because being himself without Guile, he fails to discover it in others) is apt to suffer himself to be put upon by unscrupulous Time-servers and Trimmers especially should they employ Flatterie to gain their Ends.

Before I'd made an end of Reading, I own I wept Bitter

* ie: the Popish Plot of 1678 - a malicious fabrication schemed up by a publicity-seeking hoaxer Titus Oates, and which led to nation-wide panic and persecution of many innocent Catholics.

Tears, being at last convinc'd as to the Rightness of the Doctor's Opinion, yet fall'n to so wretched a degree of Self-Reprobation even to imagine myself the Instrument of his Design. And so settl'd myself to profound thinking, and was resolv'd to conclude the matter between my Heart and what Reason counsell'd was my true Dutie. And at last perceived I ought to do as the Doctor entreated of me, for tho' it might bear the Appearance of Betrayal, yet 'twould verily be to perform a True Service for my King, if by it he might be prevented from advancing an Evil and Bloodie Enterprize.

My mind being thus resolv'd and with a Humour something more cheerfull than before, I told the Doctor that in spite of my old Sicknesse being presently upon me once again, I would do as he besought and 'twere in my power — but all in a voice so faint and languishing I could scarce myself hear the words I uttered, so that he was mov'd to ask I should repeat 'em. Then, clasping my hands in his he told me (speaking mighty earnest and civill) that I was like to the Good and Faithfull Servant in the Scriptures, that I had rightly chosen the Strait Gate and the Narrow Way, and of a Suretie I'd be rewarded in Heaven (which I own did not greatly comfort me). Then, saying he would make a beginning that self-same night of preparings against my Expedition into Scotland, and would confer with me thereon upon the morrow, the Doctor took his leave of me and so departed.

—o-o-o—

The early Spring of 1689 was a bad time for Aphra Behn – one of the most celebrated writers of her time, yet today unaccountably forgotten. (A very successful poet and playwright, she can arguably claim to be the pioneer of the novel. Her colourful track record includes a spying mission for Charles II). When her Journal opens, she is ill, in desperate financial straits, and at a low psychological ebb. Her depression – as is clear from her writings at this period, stems from failing literary inspiration, the death of many of her circle, disappointment in love, and the political disaster which had overwhelmed her patron James II. That she should agree, under these circumstances, to undertake a stressful and demanding mission, which was moreover totally inimical to her personal feelings, can only command our admiration.

2.
'A PHILOSOPHICKALL ENGINE'

London,
March 7th, 1688/9.

ALL'S NOW IN READINESS for my Journey into Scotland (rather call it Voyage for I am to set sail out of Barking in Essex on the first tide of the morrow). These past three days have seen such an infinity of divers preparations taken up that — had I not known but too well, what mighty four weeks' labour and nice management of players separate the inception of a play's rehearsing from its performance — I had doubted their accomplishment. I will set out what was done (in generall for 'twould serve but little purpose to enter into particulars) under these Severall Heads:

1. A Means of Journeying Incognito.

Doctor Burnet hath devised a Cunning Subterfuge whereby the Compleat Disappearance of A.B. shall be effected; Viz, he hath bruited it about that my sickness worsens daily apace so that I am like soon to die, and commanded that none may visit save a physician and himself. And that (a little after my departing for Scotland) my Death to be announc'd, to be follow'd by a Pompous Funerall in Westminster Abby (which the Doctor hath sufficiency of influence to carry through). These news of my Demise being spread about so publickly, I may travel in perfect Securitie that my true self will ne'er be disclosed.

2. A Disguize enabling me to mingle with All Manner of Persons their Rank notwithstanding.

My trade is to be Land-Meater* and to this end I have been furnish'd with a Letter from the Surveyor-Generall requesting that I be suffer'd without let or hindrance to examine and survey such Parks, Seats, Manors, Tenements, Woodland, Heaths, Streams, Lakes, land Arable or Waste, Messuages &c. as I desire. The Advantages whereof concerning my business of Spying being so self-evident I think, as to need no further word from me on this Head.

N.B. my rank I imagine is something betwixt a Parson's and a Gardener's (as are my clothes!) commanding a measure of respect (for such work cannot be perform'd without a degree of curious learning as Mathematicks &c.) yet smacking somewhat of the trade of a meer Mechanickall. My suppos'd business being but a Preliminarie Survey, I am spared the necessitie of acquiring such Knowledge as is proper to the Surveyor's Art, saving a little in generall sufficient to enable me to pass for that which I profess to be; neither is there need I should be cumber'd with Wands, Poles, Chains and other Impedimenta peculiar to my Office, saving a great Measuring Staff, about which more hereafter.

As to my feigning a man's part, I doubt not I'll pass that off well enow, having mingled in men's companie more than women's all my life and writ plays

* measurer

for 'em to act in. Also my suit of sad black is of sufficient looseness as not to discover the Female Form beneath.

3. Names of Persons Residing in Scotland which can be Trusted to Assist me.

Doctor Burnet hath writ for me two Letters of Introduction to two Scotch Gentlemen, both of 'em verie well-dispos'd to the Prince of Orange, Viz, Andrew Fletcher of Saltoun in Haddington-shire (which lieth not far to the eastwards of Edinburgh) also Hamilton of Biel the Lord Belhaven, of the same country which is also called East Lothiane. Both of these Lairds (as the Doctor tells me they style their lesser Nobilitie in Scotland) well known to the Doctor, especially Fletcher whose Tutor the Doctor was when he had the living of Saltoun not long after the Happy Restoration of King Charles the IInd. Fletcher is a Gentleman of great parts and many virtues (says the Doctor), tho' a most Violent Republican and extravagantly passionat. He was out with Monmouth, but shooting the Mayor of Taunton in a quarrel must needs fly to Spain, by which fortunate accident he escap'd the fatal consequences of Sedgemoor Fight. And after many Adventures, as fighting 'gainst the Turks in Hungarie, joins with William in Holland and comes over with him to Torbay, as did the Doctor himself.

The Doctor introduc'd me to a Mr. Foe, a youngish Gentleman (which was also out with Monmouth) of great wit and fine learning, and that join'd with William's army at Henley and march'd with him to London. Tho' a hose-factor (and Liveryman of the City of London) and like to do well in that way of business, I think that what chiefly engages his mind is the intercourse of persons on a larger stage as, Commerce not of Goods only, but of Ideas betwixt Nations, and Politicks for which he has a kind of Passion. He is acquainted with unnumerable persons not in England only but in the Southern Parts of Scotland also: travelling merchants who go all over the country with droves of pack-horses supplying the shops by wholesale; also buyers who give commissions to factors and warehousekeepers in London and other marts, to sell for 'em. And from this great spider's web (as 'twere) of acquaintanceship, hath supply'd me with names of merchants and shopkeepers in Edinburgh, Glasgow, Lanark, Dundee, St. John's Town* and Dunkell, all which persons would (he says) be pleased to assist me and I but make mention of his name. (How much Foe knows concerning my business in Scotland I know not, nor did I think it prudent to inquire.) From this young man I learn'd also something of the Nature of the Lord Dundee: that he is mighty scrupulous in the observance of every point in which Dutie could be said to direct him, so that being enjoined to suppress the Field-Conventicles in Galloway, became a most cruel and bloodthirsty persecutor of these poor Westland folk whose only fault (if such it can be deem'd), was to assemble in desert'd places to worship God after their own Presbyterian manner, being encourag'd to his cruel actions by spite and malice against these Hill-men, on account of they had beaten him at Drumclog Fight. And Mr. Foe went on to cite: how four men being betray'd to Claverhouse were dragg'd from their house (at a

* Perth

place call'd the Water of Dee) wherein they had been hiding, and were shot by him as they came out without any inquiry as to whether they were the persons he came to apprehend; and later, understanding the people of the town had buried 'em, caused his men to dig them up again and commanded they should lye in the fields. And how Claverhouse had with his own hand shot John Brown (a mild unoffensive man and a devout Christian), before his wife and child; how he caused to be tied to stakes in the Sollway, Margaret M'Lauchlan and Margaret Wilson, that the sea coming in drown'd 'em. And more of the same, Mr. Foe speaking with much Heat and Indignation (tho' he must have learned of these things by Report, for I do not think he was ever acquainted with Dundee).

*4. My Memorials**

In respect of my Enterprize, I am to carry through with as much Diligence and Dutifulness as I may, these Instructions following, Viz,

i. That I request and require of the aforesaid Fletcher of Saltoun that he furnish me with all the Intelligence he presently hath or may come by, concerning my Lord Dundee.

ii. That I confer with Fletcher as frequentlie as may be commode in regard to all that Dundee shall do or say at the Convention of the Estates of Scotland assembl'd in Edinburgh.

* 'Memorials' – seventeenth-century 'spy-speak' for an agent's list of instructions and requests for information from go-betweens; e.g.: the 'Memorials to Mrs Affara' which were issued to Aphra Behn at the commencement of her spying mission to Antwerp in the Dutch Wars.

iii. That I essay to learn (as much, that is, as may with Discretion and Securitie be manag'd) if Dundee hath any Private Intentions or Designs to restore King James to his Throne.

iv. That I apprise the Doctor of my Intelligence by Dispatches given into the hand of one Hezekiah Braidfute, Wright in West Bow (that being a street in Edinburgh) who will see to their sending on by certain Bearers. (And these Missives to be writ in a speciall Cypher I've been furnish'd with.)

P.S. All this to continue for as long as the Convention shall be in session; its Businesse being concluded, I am to return to London there to make Report to the Doctor.

5. Treatment for my Sicknesse.

The Doctor hath caused skilled Physicians to examine me and I have taken Physick prescribed by them; and feel a little recover'd tho' I fear 'twill not last.

6. A Conceal'd Weapon.

The Rank proper to my suppos'd trade will not permit I should go arm'd (saving a small-sword) but there hath been fashion'd for me a most ingenious piece which none may detect for 'tis incorporated within my Measuring Staff verie cunninglie in this manner: within the length of the Staff is conceal'd a gun-barrel of steel with a spiral groove which causeth the shot to spin and fly the straighter; and here's a verie curious thing, the bullet is driven not by powder but by Air, this being pump'd up into the Spherickall Knop at the head of the Staff by a lever set into the side, then releas'd by the pressing of a button. 'Twas designed by no lesser persons than Sir Robert Boyle and Sir Isaac Newton (who calls it a Philosophickall Engine) and made by one Fisher of the London Gunmakers Companie, also John Lofting a Dutchman settl'd in London and who makes fire engines.

I have made triall of it and find it shoots excellentlie well. 'Tis mighty fine; but as to the bullets, why I own I can scarce think on 'em without shame and scorn for this reason; they're cast in Silver by Sir Isaac's special instructions, he holding that there are certain persons in league with the Devil and thereby have the proof of Lead, but can be slain by Silver! 'Tis pitiful to witness the ruin of a noble intellect; they say he hath writ naught of pith or substance these twenty years and that his mind's now filled with maggots* as, Alchemy, Astrology, Sorceries and I know not what other vain superstitious Trash, now-a-days quite laid aside.

All which would be a matter rather for mirth than concern but for this: the Doctor and Mr. Foe have both related to me a belief (held only among some poor ignorant common people of Scotland to be sure, and a thing not worthie of publick credence) that Claverhouse for the reason advanc'd by Sir Isaac, had the proof of Lead and could never be slain but by a Silver Bullet. Now where did Sir Isaac learn I was to spy on a man held to be covenanted with Satan, if not from the Doctor? Such indiscretion (if indeed 'twere that – tho' I think it likely, for the Doctor's love of learning of a Secret is exeeded they say only by his love of discov'ring it to others) on the Doc-

* curious fancies

tor's part, causes me to be something troubled as to the Securitie of my Venture.

And now to report a surprizing and most Felicitous Event. At six o' clock this evening came a Gentleman in a Vizard (a fashion not so much affected now-a-days as formerly, and seldom by men); my visitor well-form'd and (what I could see beneath the Vizard) of a verie comely countenance. On my inquiring his name and business, off came the Vizard to discover the lovely face of my ador'd Mazarine, a verie Venus Unmasqued. I died* to behold her; she thank'd me mighty civill for my Dedicating of my History of the Nun to her, then we convers'd, I taking Tay while she drank Tobacco (I died to see the smoak puff prettily betwixt her lips); I died in her Embrace; O Intwin'd Extasies. Suffer me to recall here a Poem I writ some years past – To the fair Clarinda who made Love to me, imagin'd more than a Woman.

Against thy Charms we struggle but in vain,
With thy Deluding Form thou giv'st us Pain,
While the Bright Nymph betrays us to the Swain.

In pity to our Sex sure thou wer't sent
That we might love, and yet be innocent:
For sure no Crime with thee we can commit;
Or if we should – thy Form excuses it.

How much more lovable Women are than Men, and how much more worthie of Love; for to love in a Woman is to give, in a Man to take. Can it be my Love is requited? (I'm not so fond as not to see the Doctor's hand in this, he thinking perhaps to speed my Recoverie somewhat, nor

* 'went weak at the knees', to give a colloquial translation

do I think the Mazarine's Nature suffers her to be Constant in Love; yet I think her affection not entirely feign'd.) Perhaps we are to be like May-flys that love but for a day; if so 'tis enough for Astrea. And so Farewell to Love; from this day on Stern Dutie shall be Astrea's sole Mistress. Farewell Poetick Fancy — Fair Nymphs and Jolly Shepherds, Sea-Gods with Blew Locks and Shelly Trumpets, Am'rous Swains and Sighing Lovers. Farewell. Farewell.

—o-o-o—

And so, expressing herself in High Baroque imagery, Aphra Behn turns her back on Love and Poetry, to face the harsh reality of her mission at a critical watershed in her life. It may be appropriate to pause at this point in her Journal just before she enters Scotland, to look back at 1689 from the viewpoint of three centuries later, when that particular year can also be seen as a watershed. It could reasonably be objected that transcribers should stick to transcribing, and not allow themselves to be lured into the byways of historical commentary. Fair point — but on this occasion I hope I may be excused for making a few observations, as it seemed to me that the threads of Aphra Behn's life, and certain strands of History, come together at a significant moment which shows striking parallels with our own day.

In 1689, the old licentious, easy-going Cavalier society is giving place to the more 'hard-nosed' ethos of Revolution Britain with its re-emerging Puritan values of Thrift and Productiveness; similarities with the change in our own day from the Permissive Society of the 1960's and 1970's to the Enterprise Culture and 'Victorian' Values of Tory Britain are not hard to find. In Scotland in 1689, just over the horizon, far-reaching and traumatic cycles were getting ready to turn

– the destruction of Gaeldom (Glencoe to the Clearances via Culloden), the erosion of Scottish identity. Recent signs however suggest that these cycles may have almost run their course: for the first time in centuries Gaelic has stopped receding; there is a new positive mood of Scottish consciousness. Looking back at 1689 from the 1990's one has an extraordinary sense of 'déjà vu', of 'This is where I came in'. This feeling is heightened by the fact that the period has seen the long Imperial adventure come and go, and society change from a pre- to a post-Industrial one. So in a sense it could almost be said we are back where we started in 1689, and sharing something of the same perspective. Perhaps History really does repeat itself in cycles.

The tall Scots Pines which form such a landmark on the eastern flank of North Berwick Law, and which were planted in the year of Union, have recently been reported to be nearing the end of their life. Coincidence – or a prophetic symbol? Time will tell.

3.

' A LOW THIN MAN, EYES FULL OF FIRE '

Edinburgh,
March 13th, 1688/9.

THERE BE TWO CAUSES why I've delay'd to write in my Journall these five days, Viz, what with incessant journeyings and discourse I have had but scant Leisure, and was also so much incommoded by the Motion of the vessel on the voyage that I fancy'd I was like to die, moreover being so wearied and so sleepy had but little inclination to attend to any dutie save what was wholly needful. But now, being safe arriv'd in Edinburgh and install'd in lodgings, I shall set down without further delay what has occur'd in the mean time.

Having taken my farewell of the Doctor on the 7th at a late hour, I journeyed to Barking in a Hackney-coach while it was yet night, being accompanied thither by a Mr. Wm. Carstares – a large, fair-complected mild-mannered Scotchman of amiable Disposition and the trusted secretarie of the Prince (being his Spymaster-Generall while the Invasion was a-readying). Tho' I damn'd his politicks here was a man I could yet admire for tho' put to long and cruel torture by the Prince's enemies, never a word would he utter to betray his Master and be spared the torment. (This I had from the Doctor.) From this gallant gentleman I learn'd which persons were to attend the Convention, of each his Humour, what his Party and affections, as: the Duke of Hamilton (who is like to become the President of the Convention) tho' a brave man in a pass is the veryest coward when call'd on to give opinion or counsell, for he will mean one thing at ten o' clock and another at noon, like unto the Chameleon which changes his colour with his resting-place; whether for fear of offending, or of committing himself to an enterprize and not be able to draw back therefrom, none can say. And John Dalrymple, the Earl Stair, a cunning unforgiving man of infinite malice 'gainst any who cross him (and a fawning time-server to boot who, tho' a Whig and privy to William's Design, yet play'd his personage on King James to such effect as to supplant for a space, Sir Geo. MacKenzie in the office of Lord Advocat). Carstares adviz'd me I should put in at Berwick, for the Governor of that place hath always fresh Intelligence of what's afoot in Scotland, and moreover has a kind of Privy Purse with which to encourage English spies.

But that was not to be for we made such an excellent fast Passage, the wind blowing fair all the while that the Master of the vessel (a Barking smack) prevail'd on me to agree 'twere wiser to press on while the wind was yet in our favour, with which advice I could not but concur being in something of a fret to reach Edinburgh before the Convention should assemble. (These Barking Fisher-smacks are such wonderful good sailers they're verie useful to the publick on many occasions; as particularly in time of War they're used as Press-smacks, as in the late Dutch Wars, running to all the northern coasts to man the Navy when any Expedition is at hand that requires a sudden Equipment.)

And so at about four o' clock in the morning of the 12th, we came to off Dunbar at the entrance to the Firth or Aestuarium of the Forth River, the Master unwilling to run into the Harbour (it lying in the midst of dangerous rocks) so that I was set down with my dunnage by the Harbour-wall from the vessel's skiff. I dallied awhile beside the Harbour (which was built by the usurper Oliver after he had defeated the Scots here; some say in amends for that ill turn) until the North Port (as the Scots call their Town Gates) should be opened and the townspeople to go about their business, as not wishing to bring attention to myself. And thus by and by find myself inside the Town, a handsome well-built place and the first I was ever in in Scotland, the houses curiously align'd with their gables ends facing onto the Street, of which there is but one (tho' verie fine and broad to be sure) for the narrow lanes betwixt the houses scarce deserve the name of such.

I broke my fast at a hostelrie, where I own I felt verie dash'd and in the Dumps, in part from Fatigue but more from a black heavie Melancholie concerning my appointed Task, also feeling myself to be an utter Stranger in a Foreign Land. For tho' Dunbar is not above twenty or thirty mile from English ground 'tis as perfectly Scots (so it appear'd to me) as if you might be 100 miles north of Edinburgh, nor is there the least appearance of any thing English, nor any English person, neither customs nor usages (saving that they speak English tho' in a Dialect of their own) any more than if they had never heard of an English Nation.

I made inquiry where I might purchase a nag, also as to directions for the way to Biel where I purpos'd to introduce myself to the Lord Belhaven. Thus, having set my hand to the plough-stilts as 'twere, I began to rail against myself for being cast down and showing so poor a Spirit and bethought myself how others which had infinitely heavier loads to bear than mine, had yet acquitted themselves worthwhilie, as Carstares, who had remained silent under torture tho' he had no cause to hope for any deliverance soever, or Fletcher who for no other cause than Chivalrie had taken Monmouth's part, tho' knowing he must fail. And so, something more cheerful, I departed from Dunbar by the West Port, carrying my portmanteau and with my staff in my hand, on the High Road that leads west towards Edinburgh.

My spirits continu'd to lift at my first sight of the Country of Scotland for (in this Parte at the least) saving that 'tis not so much enclos'd, it appear'd as fruitful and pleasant almost as most places in England; on the right hand at a little distance the Firth with a great rock called the Bass standing high out of the Water, and on the left Mountains at a greater distance. These hills (which my Map tells me are called Lammyr Moor) are not extremely high, not barren but passable and habitable and have large flocks of sheep feeding and many open roads lie over 'em. At a little scatter'd place call'd West Barns I sought out a certain fellow (which had been recommended to me in Dunbar) and from him bought a Bay Horse with saddle and other necessarie gear; then a little way on at a habitation called Beltonfoord bent my course towards the hills, that is to the south, and soon came to Biel, a noble house consisting of an ancient Pele with some modern work join'd thereto, and set in a Park amid pleasant groves and walks of trees (as it would appear are many of the noblemen's houses in Lothiane).

My Lord Belhaven being at home, after he had read the Doctor's letter, receiv'd me verie graciouslie; a well favour'd black* man verie amiable tho' something vain, and at times tedious in his discourse which dwelleth overmuch on the historie of Scotland. He purpos'd (he said) to begin his Journey to Edinburgh to attend the Convention this verie day and would be pleased and I wish'd to accompanie him to Yester where he was to pass

* dark-eyed and dark-complexioned

the night.

Soon we were on our way, keeping to the fine and pleasant Vale of a River call'd Tyne (which I shall name the Scots Tyne to distinguish it from the Tyne in Northumberland, tho' the inhabitants thereabouts not knowing any other do not so distinguish it) which runs by Haddington, the Shire Town (as 'twould be call'd in England) and what they call here a Royal Burgh (which is much what we call a Corporation in England). 'Tis a handsome old, decay'd place with a good stone bridge over the Tyne and a vast ancient Church sadly ruin'd. My Interest was much quicken'd to learn from my companion that in this Church is a Chappel and Burial Place of the Maitlands (for you should know that the Dedication of my book Oroonoko is to Richard Maitland of that verie Family). Here we cross'd the Tyne and passing by Lethington* the ancient home of the Maitlands (that is, until but seven years ago when John Maitland, Duke of Lauderdale, which had for a by-name the UNCROWN'D KING of Scotland, died) and arriv'd at Yester the Seat of the Earl of Tweed-dal; where is a verie splendid Park with fine Vistas and Avenues, the love of managing which the Earl took in from King Charles II, my Lord Belhaven inform'd me.

Here we parted verie friendly, he urging me verie earnest to call upon him should I ever need Assistance (which caused me to reflect that the Doctor's Letter must needs touch on Weightie Matters – but in such fashion, I sincerelie hoped, as not to discover my Business to others; this reflexion doth bring me some Concern, tho' thus far I confess I've no just cause). As to Fletcher (says my Lord), whom now you are to visit, he is a gentleman steadie in his Principles, of Nice Honour, brave as the sword he

* now called Lennoxlove

wears and bold as a lion. He would lose his life readily to serve his Country, and would not do a Base Thing to save it.

And now turning my face to the west I arriv'd after a few miles at Saltoun Hall hard by a hamlet of the same name. (I should in Scotland call such a place a Town, according to the proper Usage of their speech, for here the meanest villages are so nam'd, even the verie farm-dwellings!) I reflected with some gratification that none had thus far doubted my Guise as a Man; I own this had caused me to be something troubled at the first, but as my appearance was everiewhere accepted for that which it feign'd to be, my unease by little and little wore off so that by the time I was come to Saltoun, I could play the part with such Ease and Naturalness as not to be troubled with any more doubts, no not one.

At a gate in the stone-wall by which the House is enclos'd, I was accosted by an old rusty fellow who conducted me through a fine Park not, to my astonishment, unto the Hall itself (a Noble Pile of no vast antiquitie, four square and massy yet verie fine and elegant withal), but to a modest dwelling call'd the Dowery-House some little way off. My name being sent up to Fletcher, by and by I was sent for up, and receiv'd by that gentleman with much civilitie. (Truly these Scotch gentry are so hospitable, so courteous, so addicted to improve their estates that none in England, nay in Europe, better deserve the name of Gentlemen.)

The Laird of Saltoun is a low* thin man of brown complection, Eyes full of Fire, with a Piercing Look. After having read the Doctor's Letter, Fletcher claps me on the shoulder verie friendly and asks in affectionate terms how his old Tutor did. And then walks with me in the Park,

* short

and by and by we are come to a Declivity above a little River which made the softest murmurs and purlings in the world, and the opposite bank was adorn'd with quantities of curious Shrubs and Trees of a thousand rare forms, that the Prospect was the most pleasing that Art and Nature together could create and, but that the season was not yet sufficientlie advanc'd for shoots and flowers to appear (saving pretty Daffydils which did besprinkle all the ground) would have been ravishing.

I told Fletcher how fine and pleasing I thought his House and Estate to be, whereupon he reply'd something bitter they were not yet his, that in consequence of his having run fortunes with Monmouth they'd been made forfeit, that in Law they yet belong'd to the Earl of Dumbarton whose agent for them was his (the Earl's) brother, the Duke of Hamilton, he who looked fair to become President of the Convention.

—And so I visit here on suff'rance, (cry'd Fletcher) —in spite of all my Labours in Holland in the Cause of the Prince which is now King William and has not as good a right to his Crown as I have to my Estate.

I then asked Fletcher (more to make Conversation than for other cause) did he purpose to attend the Convention? Which inquiry appear'd to vex him exceedinglie for his Eyes flash'd Fire (as 'twere) and he reply'd verie hot and violent he had not been Summon'd but would yet go to Edinburgh, and Devil take him if he'd not find Ways and Means they should hear and weigh his Counsell.

Truly I was mov'd to Pitie for this good man whose misfortunes seem'd to derive more from his putting Service to others above Profit to himself than for other cause. And moreover this unselfish Nobilitie of Character e'en caused him to be misluck'd in Love, for while he sojourned Abroad a Fugitive and Proscribed Traitor, his Lady Love Margaret Carnegie was woo'd and won by his own brother Henry. (This I had from the Doctor.) Which (now that I had met with Fletcher) was to me no great wonder, for a Comelie Face join'd with Flatt'ring Attentions, tender looks of Love, Trembling Sighs and Billets-doux, will win a Woman's Heart more surely than Nobleness and Virtue be they never so great; and for a suretie Fletcher's form and face would ne'er advance his Suit at Cupid's Bar!

That same afternoon, Fletcher being desirous of reaching Edinburgh before noon of the morrow, we journey'd to Tranent, passing the great House of Winton where we turned aside out of our way to view the Seat with its Park and Gardens, which the Earl Seton show'd to us verie hospitably, and show'd us also a new book call'd The Scots Gardener writ by one John Reid, full of sound and curious Precepts which the Earl was presently making triall of, to much good effect as we could for ourselves see. Indeed there are abundance of Gentlemen's Seats and ancient Mansions whose possessions are large in this country of East Lothiane.

—Which Gentry (said Fletcher) —are fam'd for the most part as being men of Honour and Right Principle, who in the late times of Tyrrany and Crueltie scrupled not to oppose the Arbitrary Designs of firstly, the Duke of Lauderdale, then the Duke of York on his becoming the Administrator of Scotland, as: the Lord Yester, Sinclair of Stevenston, Murray of Blackbarronnie, Baillie of Jerviswood, Cockburn of Ormiston, &c. (saving only those two Time-servers Hepburn of Humbie and Wedderburn of Gosford).

—But Lauderdale and the Duke of York which is now King James II, (I was mov'd to protest) —were but carrying through the Policies of our rightfull King, Charles II.

—By whose Authoritie, Rightfull? demands Fletcher waxing passionate.

—Why by God's, (I return'd with some Heat for I own Fletcher's words rankled somewhat) —and by Hereditary Principle.

—Now that is an Impeccable Argument! declares Fletcher in Scorn, —so then we may see with just cause Hereditary Professors of Divinitie in our Colleges!

To which I return'd a soft Answer and bit my lip (as the saying is) it being none of my purpose to provoke Fletcher, but rather the opposite. But all this by the way; I do but relate it to show the manner of man Fletcher is, and what his Humour.

By and by I ventur'd to inquire what were my companion's Thoughts concerning the Lord Dundee, (I own I ask'd this with some Trepidation quite expecting Fletcher to blaze out in a passion, Eyes flashing Fire, &c.). But surely the name of Dundee touched on Matters too Deep and Weightie for meer Huffing and Ire, for he reply'd in a low small voice,

—That man will and he is able, put a Noose around the necks (and mine the foremost) of such gentrie as have oppos'd the Tyrant James, and will busy himself by all the Means he hath to restore his Master to his Throne when, should such Ill Chance come to pass, farewell Libertie.

—But is not such Loyaltie giv'n by a Subject to his Liege a Thing rather to be commended than cried down? I could not forbear to ask.

—A King is owed but the Loyaltie he deserves of, return'd Fletcher. —When King John Balliol betray'd his Nation to Edward of England, did the Scots scruple to put him aside and choose Wallace as their guardian? And shall we scruple to put James aside and choose William for our King at the Convention? If we do other (tho' 'tis scarce conceivable we should) then all poor Scotland's Suff'rings and Resistances these fifty years were in vain and the Blood of her Martyrs spil't to no Purpose.

Thus, having ascertain'd that Fletcher's Opinion as to Dundee's Intentions concurr'd pretty well with the Doctor's, I was the more convinc'd of their Truth and so was well enow content there to let the Matter rest.

Having pass'd the night in Tranent (tho' a Royal Burgh and its inhabitants as industrious and laborious as any to be seen in England from the abundance of coal-pits round about, 'tis but an indifferent place) we turn'd to our left a little, the High Road being exceeding Mirey, holding to a road they call hereabouts Birsley Brae (Brae signifying an Incline, in their Dialect) which led us to the Summit of a ridge nam'd Falside Hill from the Castle there (now ruin'd from taking fire but a few years past). From this eminence we could clearly see a range of small towns standing thick upon the coast, Viz, Seaton, Cockenny, Salt Preston, &c. Here we fell in with a great throng of a Vagabond sort of People, clad in rags for the most part, many of them drunk, cursing and shouting in a most Horrid Manner, the most ill-looking set of Rogues I ever saw in my life and a great wonder to me, for such a Sight has not been seen in England since Queen Elizabeth's time I warrant. Whether they intended us a Mischief or no I cannot say, but we rode steadfastlie on looking neither to the right nor to the left, which I think may have deterr'd 'em somewhat, and so got past (or through, rather I should say for they quite filled up the road and scorn'd to give place) without scathe saving a brisk Bombardment of Oaths, which Artillery-shot I minded not at all. Being at last clear of 'em, out bursts Fletcher in a Passion, calling them murtherous incestuous Ruffians and a Curse upon the face of Scotland, able-bodied beggars which would do no work instead molesting and affrighting honest Folk who were thereby compell'd to pay and feed them to begone.

—Sell them to the Plantations or ship them to Venice to fight against the Turks! cry'd Fletcher.

—Would you then restore Slaverie? I ask'd, something astonied that Fletcher the Champion of Libertie and the self-sworn Foe of Tyrants should express such Sentiments.

—Aye, would I, (declares he) —if that be the Means to cure the Nation of this great and continuing Ill. I deal in Things not Words; when these marauding Vagabonds, full one tenth part of the inhabitants of Scotland, live like Leeches by sucking the blood of the rest, I do not scruple to advize a Sharp Remedie.

But to discourse of Slaverie is one thing, to witness it another, as we were soon to find. For by and by, descending down a steep face of this Falsyde Hill, we came among Coal-pits, our road taking us so near the verie edge of one we would fain peer in, which was much the same I should guess, as if we were to view the Infernal Region itself. For O what a Horrid and Melancholie Sight was here; women and even little children bow'd beneath great baskets of Coals, heaving themselves with infinite Pain and Difficultie up long ladders propt upon ledges one below the other, and descending to a Vast Depth clean out of our sight into Pitch-Darknesse, where only little flick'ring points of light from their candles mark'd the toilers' Upward Progress. And as these miserable Wretches struggl'd on the rungs some groan'd, some wept most bitterly, some cry'd aloud in their Distresse, like so many tormented Souls in Hell.

Even as we gazed into the Pit a lad (of twelve or thirteen years I guess) clamber'd out of the mouth thereof and being, on account of the Exremitie of his Exhaustion, unable to stand upright made shift to crawl upon his hands and knees like to a four-footed Beast of Burden, his Destination a great Heap of Coals some thirty or forty yards distant. Then with a little start did I perceive two singular things:

1, that the boy was Black, and this not from the Coal-Dust but on account of Black was his Naturall Hue, he was in other words a Negroe; and

2, around his neck was affix'd a Brazen Collar just such as you may see on a Bear or other Chain'd Beast. On inquiring of Fletcher what such an Article might signify, he reply'd (something abash'd I thought) that 'twas a Serf-Collar.

—Why then, are these poor people Slaves! I ask'd.

—In every point save Name, reply'd he, —for though they earn wages they belong to their Master utterly, and cannot under Law leave his Employ; and should the Mine change hands are sold and bought with the Pit Furniture.

—Such Barbarousness I never heard of! I exclaim'd: —Why the Last Serf in England by name John Pigge died near a hundred years past, and even in his time was a great Wonder; as he might be the Last Druid or the Last Dragon-Slayer or some such.

Just then I perceiv'd that the young Negroe, quite overcome with his Exertions and the great weight of his Burden, was fall'n upon his side, yet even in that Posture essayed to drag himself along (with many of his Coals being spill'd) gasping and moaning most piteouslie.

—Come Sir, I beseech'd Fletcher, —this is past bearing, let us help the poor lad.

Fletcher, who I think was as much mov'd as myself, for his long Face was all a-working, made haste to dismount, as I had, and assisted me in lifting the Basket of Coals from the lad's back, and a mighty Labour we had of it to haul the load to the Heap where the Coals were laid out to be sold. But on turning around to return to where we had left our horses standing, we espied a rough fellow a-kicking and belabouring the poor Black who yet lay on the ground. Enrag'd, I ran up and lifting a Coal from the ground cast it with all my might at the lad's Tormentor. The Coal smote him upon the side of his Head so that he reel'd, then whirling about he espies whence came the Buffet, and with a Horrid Oath makes to return it with his Fist. Then:

—Hold Rogue! cry's Fletcher, and plucking forth his Sword, in a Fury smites the fellow with the flat thereof severall times, that he falls back something cow'd. The Blackamoor being now arisen attempts bravely to smile and in a faint voice thanks Fletcher and myself, but then says it had been better we had not intervened as his punishment must now be many times the greater.

Whereat Fletcher begins sharply to question the other, by which we learn'd: that he was a Hewer and the boy his Frem'd Bearer, by which he meant that being unmarried he had no Wife nor Children to bear away the Coals he hewed (which Labour they perform for no Wages) and so must needs hire a Stranger to do this Task; that his Bearer being tardy in returning, he had himself ascended to the Pit Mouth to see what was amiss; and finding his Bearer a-shirking of his Dutie sees fit to chastise him. (This is to give but the sense of his Discourse, for his Speech, or Dialect rather, was so violent, so coarse, so broken with foul Oaths and they so many, that 'twould serve but little purpose to set down an Exact Rendering.)

For myself, I could in no wise endure that the poor Blackamoor lad should remain a day longer in the Service of this Brute, no not one, and roundly declar'd he must make shift to find himself another Bearer for I intended to remove the Negroe from this Place. At which the Hewer broke out that the Law would not suffer I should do so, that the Negroe had been sold to the Pit Owner and Arles taken, (meaning that the Vendor had accepted a Gift or Payment to seal the Bargaine) and was thus his Propertie as a Perpetuall Servant.

—Be that as it will, I said, —the lad comes with me and that be his wish.

At which the Blackamoor implores me with Piteous Intreaties (as would have mov'd a Stone) that he be suffered to accompanie me. And all the while this Disputation rag'd Bearers with their Baskets full and empty passed and re-passed by us, so sunk in their own Miserie as not to pay us any Heed at all.

Well, the long and the short of the Matter was that in a little space we three, Viz, Fletcher, myself and the Negroe Boy were proceeding on our way, leaving behind us one sore perplex'd and verie angry Collier, and having, as 'twere set fire to a Powder-train which must sooner or later cause the Blowing-up of a Petard.

To myself I own'd 'twas monstrous Folly to have acted so, it being nothing to my Purpose and indeed like to cause me vast Trouble and Hindrance should the Pit-owner find me to re-claim his Propertie. Yet I could not find it in my Heart to regret what I had done, the more so when Fletcher prais'd me verie warmly saying 'twas the Act of a Gentleman to put my hand in the Fire for a Stranger's Sake, especially it being done for Charitie alone, and myself having no Profit in the matter. It is writ in Holy Scripture: Sufficient unto the Day is the Evil thereof; and, Cast thy Bread upon the Waters; likewise, Take no Thought for the Morrow; the remembrance of which Maxims comforted me somewhat.

On my asking the lad what was his Name, he reply'd 'twas Caesar (which Disclosure did cause me to start; the cause whereof I shall explain by and by), and being press'd as to how he had come by such Outlandish Appellation, related to us the Historie of his short Life which I here set down just as he told us, tho' putting my own Interpretation upon his words where their Meaning might not otherwise be entirely clear:

He had been born a Black-slave on the Island of Jamayca while Morgan the Buccaneer was yet Deputy Governor of that Place, his Master a kind Gentleman who used him well, training him to wait at Table, to run Errands about the Plantation, to accompanie him as he went about his Businesse as a kind of Running Footman, to lay out his Cloths; and in a word to be as much Companion as Servant. Also, this good man his Master, being himself without Issue, delighted in nothing more than to instruct young Caesar ('tis a Fancy of the Whites in our West-India Colonies to name their Slaves after celebrated Ancients, as; Pompey, Scipio Africanus, &c.) not only in Reading and Writing, but in Geographie and Histories, the Use of the Globes, Mathematicks, French and Latin.

His Master had, 'twould appear, but one Fault, but that of such a Grievous Nature as on its own to be sufficient to undo him, which was to play intemperately at Cards; while engag'd in this Pastime he would be seiz'd with an Ungovernable Madnesse as 'twere, causing him to play on tho' losing more than his Purse could easily bear. And on one especiall Occasion, having made shift to get so mightily into debt as not to be able to pay all in Specie and in Bond, he must needs part with Caesar for whom his Gaming-partner (a Scotch Gentleman) had conceiv'd a mighty Fancy, declaring he would accept Caesar in the Room of what was yet owed him.

And so, Caesar having exchang'd Masters, by and by accompanied this Scotch Gentleman when he return'd to his Seat in the Western Highlands; here was Caesar much admir'd and lov'd by all persons of the Household, on account of being so apt to learn, so modest and so charming. But then, his Master on account of being out with Argyle (in the late Rebellion) was attainted and his Estate and Goods declar'd Forfeit, with the unhappy

Consequence for Caesar that he was purchas'd by the York-Buildings Companie along with other Stock and after sold to a Pit-owner for a Perpetuall Servant, in which Estate we found him.

(—Which, declar'd Fletcher, —touch'd on a Nice Point of Law, Viz, there being no such thing as Slaverie known in Scotland, could a person even tho' he be a minor, be sold into Serfdom as a consequence of his being a Slave — if his Slaverie was in Law Null and Void?)

But I promis'd to tell you why the mention of his Name should occasion me Surprize. Well, you should know that the hero of my book *Oroonoko* (which was publish'd but a year past, and which I have had occasion already to make mention of) was likewise nam'd Caesar (tho 'twas Oroono-ko in his own country of Coromantien which is in Africa), he too being a Black-slave — no feign'd Hero but a real Person whom I was privileg'd to know as a Friend when I liv'd in Surinam.

—Well young Sir, I said, when the Blackamoor had done telling us his Historie, —I think Caesar but a sorry Name for such a fine lad as yourself, and tho' giv'n in Rememb'rance of a Great and Famous Man, serves but as a constant Reminder of a Servile Estate. Would'st not rather have an honest Christian Name?

—Why Sir, right gladly, (says he, mighty eager).

—Then, and you be willing, I shall call you Samuel, which signifies Heard of God, for I think perhaps we both in our Hearts called on the Lord this Day and that he hearkened unto us. (There be some may object that Samuel being a Name used among the Hebrews, 'tis not a Christian Name but that were a Meer Quibble; Alexan-der and Hector are likewise Names commonly used among Christians yet are from the Pagan Greeks.) Whereat Samuel (for I shall hereafter call him none other) reaches up and with tears in his eyes clasps me by the hand, which

Action moves me so, that for a little space after I am constrained to Silence.

But now we are come to Musselbro, a populous Town or rather three Towns all built together, Viz, Musselbro proper, Inneresk, and Fisheraw or the row of houses where the Fishermen usually dwell; for here is still many Fishermen and was formerly many more when the Mussel-fishing was accounted a Valuable Thing, but now 'tis given over tho' the mussels lie on the shore in vast quantities. From hence we had but five miles to Edinburgh but on account of the View of the Citie from the east being verie confused (because of its breadth being but ill-proportioned to its length which runs from east to west), on Fletcher advising it we turn'd out of our way a little to the right hand towards Leith, and so came towards the Citie from the north and a mighty fine Prospect it was, with a Palace call'd Holyroodhouse standing upon flat low ground at the eastern Extremitie, then a long row of tall buildings upon a Ridge, which gradually ascending ends at the west in a Vast Crag, of which the side facing us is a Frightfull Precipice and is surmounted by a great and (to all appearance) impregnable Castle; and below the Castle at the foot of this Precipice is a Lake (or Loch as they call it) of standing water.

Fetching a little sweep to the right hand as to leave Holyroodhouse on our left, we entered into the Palace precincts at an entrance which is called the Water Port, and by and by found ourselves in a Great Street going in a straight line east and west, and bearing to the right again (that is to say to the west) begin to climb the Ridge. Tho' this Part is but a suburb (and is called the Cannon-Gate) it has yet some verie magnificent houses of the Nobilitie. Then, entering into the Citie properly so call'd by a Gate call'd the Nether-Bow Port, we find this same Great Street continuing, only wider than before, close-pack'd on either side with houses of a Prodigious Height rising to seven, ten, even twelve Storey high, and between the houses steep lanes they call Wynds falling away to north and south so sudden as must greatly incommode those which walk in them. And in this Street are two great Churches, The Trone-Kirk which is pretty modern and the High Kirk of St. Giles, a Gothic Pile. Here also are many fine Publick Buildings as: their Parliament House and the places for assemblie of their College of Justice, Exchequer, Justiciary, &c. Truly I think that for its length, its size and the Splendour of its Buildings this Street must be the finest not in Britain only but in the World.

After consulting with me where and when we should meet on the morrow, Fletcher finds me stabling and (after we had purchas'd a decent suit of clothes for Samuel and had a Smith file off his Collar) lodging for Samuel and myself in that part of the High Street call'd the Land-Market* a little below the Castle. I was much astonied at finding upon the common stair of the building Persons from all Ranks of Society coming and going and moreover, greeting each other verie civilly and familiarly, a thing surely never to be seen or heard of in England. After Samuel and myself had shar'd a chine of Mutton and a flask of Claret by way of supper, we were soon abed, Samuel upon a little truckle and myself in a bed within a tiny room built into the verie wall! (Methinks that the Scots tho' in many points a most Admirable Nation, do maintain some passing strange Usages.) So ended my second day in Scotland.

* Aphra Behn means the Lawn Market

4.

'...GRANT WARRANT TO REQUIRE HIM TO REMOVE OUT OF THE SAID CASTLE...'*

Edinburgh,
March 16th, 1688/9.

GREAT EVENTS happen daily apace in this Citie, some witness'd by myself, some I have by Report from Fletcher who tho' himself disbarr'd the Convention is yet Privy to much of its Businesse by reason that so many of his friends are in the Assemblie; Fletcher being generally held in much Affection and Regard. Fletcher stays with friends in the Cow-Gate (already I am something fall'n into their Manner of Speech, for they say, stay, where we would say, live) and I meet with him daily, he addressing me as Mr. Tom Johnson, which Cognomen was to me the easiest and most Naturall Thing in the world to devize for I did but borrow its Parts from the names of my old friend and Benefactor Sir Thos. Gower and of my Father Bartholomew Johnson.

Our Rendez-Vous is the Piazza where the merchants foregather and is next their Parliament-House (where the Convention tho' 'tis not properly a Parliament, assembles), and if the hour be late we repair from the Piazza

* Proceedings of the Estates of Scotland, 1689

unto TIBBIE JOHNSTONE'S, a Tavern hard by, and is methinks a meeting-place for all the World and fam'd for all manner of Gossip, News, Discourse and Conversation; here and you will, you may find a Nobleman with his boots being mended by a Cobbler and the Pair arguing Theology as expertly as any Professors in the Schools. The News of what's toward or happening I hear from Fletcher almost as soon as he hears them himself and so have been enabl'd to send Dispatches to the Doctor furnishing him with prompt Intelligence. (Fletcher being so free with me, I begin to think the Doctor hath told him pretty plain in his Letter what my Businesse here is.) And these Matters I now enumerate as following:

1. To speak in generall of how Matters stand in Edinburgh in this present Pass, the Town is much disorder'd with Whiggish Mobs from the West, followers of the Duke of Hamilton, which roam around as they will, openly arm'd, none daring to check 'em, abusing and affrighting Cavaliers and Prelatists, as they call them that adhere to Episcopacy (which until these present Troubles was the Establish'd Form of Worship in Scotland tho' much misliked by the greater part of the Populace), and seeking next whom they should Rathillet, as they say. (I should explain that Hackston of Rathillet was one of that Covenanting Band who in 1679 encompass'd the Murther of Archbishop Sharpe whom they held to be a great Oppressor of the poor, common, Presbyterian Folk; for which murther was this Hackston of Rathillet later apprehended and executed with much Crueltie, his hands being first cut off. And so there is now made a new Verb Transitive, Viz, to Rathillet, which signifies to be reveng'd upon.) And besides this Rabble of Clydes-Dale Hill-men, 'tis ru-

mour'd there is severall Companies of Foot-Soldiers brought in by Hamilton and presently conceal'd in Garretts and Cellars, they being unable to be quarter'd in the Castle by reason that the Duke of Gordon presently holds that Fortress for King James.

2. Upon this last Foot; the Duke of Gordon is (so Fletcher tells me) a man weak and wavering in Courage but bound by Shame and Religion, and, upon receipt of a Letter of Indemnity from the Prince of Orange and further, being requir'd by the Earls of Lothiane and Tweed-dall under Warrant from the Convention on the first day of its assembling Viz, 14th March, that he evacuate the Castle, was in the verie Act of removing his Goods and Dunnage from that Place (having held it for King James since December) when my Lord Dundee makes shift to enter into the Castle, and play'd his Personage upon the Duke to such effect as to stiffen his Resolution that he draws back into the Castle like a Snaile into his Shell. And on the next day, that being the 15th March, the Convention is mighty amaz'd and annoy'd to find the Castle once more shut fast against 'em. And declaring Gordon did but trifle with 'em, sends up Heralds which proclaim the Duke of Gordon to be a Traitor. And now is the Castle quite block'd up and invested.

3. Upon this sixteenth day of March was read to the Lords of the Convention assembl'd in Parliament-House, two letters; the first being from the Prince of Orange, the second from King James, the Prince's

full of Smooth and Comfortable* Words design'd to allay all Subjects' Fears, and which was receiv'd with marks of Gratitude and Respect. But upon the King's Letter being read (by one Crane, a Servant of the Queen) then was heard a Noise and Humming throughout the House, and when the reading was done, there burst out a Roar of Triumph and Mockerie from the Whigs, but those which supported King James remain'd silent and abash'd, being quite put out of Countenance. For the Letter was Haughty and Ireful in Manner, threat'ning the Convention with Punishment in this World and Damnation in the next. 'Tis thought the Letter was writ by the Duke of Melfort who has much influence with the King, and that it was preferr'd above a Draft (full of Reconciliation, Dignity and Moderateness 'tis said) sent by My Lord Dundee to King James. If 'twere so, then Melfort hath done the King a greater Dis-service than even his bitterest Enemies could contrive, for now 'tis certain the Convention will choose William to be King in Scotland.

N.B. Tho' I am sensible of the Necessitie that King James be not encourag'd with False Hopes of recov'ring his Throne, I own these News did come near to cause my Heart to break.

P.S. At this time occurr'd an Affaire which 'twere easy to dismiss as Trifling Foolerie, but which I fear may yet have Ill Consequences for the perusal of my Task; so I'll apprise you of it.

Now there was in this Tibbie Johnstone's tavern I spake of, a serving-wench call'd Meg not ill-favour'd but passing bold and saucie (what we would call a Hussy but they

* Reassuring.

term a Besom — which likewise signifies a Broom!) that show'd a mighty interest in my Person, ever (to my considerable Vexation) finding some cause or other to attend upon me, inquiring was the Ale brewed to my liking? Did I wish my seat drawn nearer the Ingle? &c., all which Civillities were, it seem'd to me, but feign'd; meer Contrivances to learn what were my Humour, Speech and Manners. Tho' Fletcher, conceiving the Jade to be enamour'd of me, did find my Discomfiture vastly diverting; for myself, I was something concern'd — that her Attentions were occasion'd by another cause altogether, Viz, suspicion that I was no Man but a Woman aping such.

And in this surmise was I proved aright; one evening as I sate alone in the tavern a-waiting for Fletcher I call'd for Claret, which this Meg brings, then returning with my change cries, —Kep! (Which is to say, Catch) and casts the coins in my lap. Having no leisure to consider the action proper to my feign'd Sex, I open my knees (which is Naturall to a Woman, she thinking to catch 'em in her Skirts; whereas a Man would close his knees that the coins not fall between). What a Ringing and Rolling of Coin now ensu'd, what a Humming and Mirth among the Companie!

Mighty abash'd, I make shift to gather up the scatter'd Placks, Bodles, &c. (for you should know that both as to Value and Denomination their coinage differs from ours), and while I am engag'd in this Task observe two Men to arise and take their leave. Being so distracted in my mind, I paid this occurrence but scant heed at the time, but after, reflecting on the matter, it seem'd to me they did nod to each other as tho'confirmed in some Opinion. Which did cause me to inquire of myself; were they Spies of the Jacobite Party that had learn'd of my Businesse and had employ'd Meg to discover my true Sex to them? Perchance these Fears of mine be Baseless; nevertheless I own my mind is something troubl'd thereby.

5.

'... THE LORD VISCOUNT OF DUNDEE HAD A CONFERENCE WITH THE DUKE OF GORDON AT THE POSTERN GATE OF THE CASTLE ...'*

Edinburgh,
March 19th, 1688/9.

EVENTS NOW FALL so thick upon each other and have assum'd such an Untoward Cast that, like a mariner which of a sudden hath lost his Bearings, I am sore perplex'd as to what Course I must now follow. Since last I writ in my Journall, these following has transpired:

1. My Lord Dundee hath complained in the House of a Plot to murther him and Sir Geo. MacKenzie both, and says moreover he will show the verie house wherein his intending murtherers lie conceal'd, that they may be brought to justice; but 'tis cry'd up in the Convention, Hamilton declaring they could not postpone Publick Affairs to consider Private Businesse.

* Proceedings of the Estates of Scotland, 1689.

2. Dundee is today departed out of the Citie! I saw him at the head of a Troop of Horse gallop through the streets; and a friend calling out to him to know whither he went he wav'd his hat and cry'd back (mighty gallant and cheerfull),

—Wherever the Spirit of Montrose shall direct me!

Beholding him, I started in Amaze; could this be the Monster of Crueltie which had pistoll'd poor ignorant Dissenting Folk before their Wives and Children, as hath been reported to me? He had the noblest Port* and most Comelie Form of any man I ever yet beheld, an Oval Face (fram'd in curling locks) perfectlie form'd, of an Expression both Sweet and Grave, and of such Surpassing Glorious Beauty as would cause Adonis or Apollo to be consum'd with Envie. (Yet Lucifer 'tis said, was also Fair of Face.) My old Sicknesse troubling me somewhat, I retired to my Lodgings there to rest awhile (Samuel going to the Apothecarie to fetch me Physick; he is mighty diligent in the performance of small Menial Duties, as sweeping the chamber, fetching water from the Wells in the Cow-Gate, brushing and laying out clothes, &c., needing never to be ask'd and does such Service willingly and cheerfully).

By and by, being something recover'd and the time of my meeting with Fletcher drawing nigh, I set out from my lodgings. And find the Citie in an Uproar with Drums a-beating and Trumpets blowing and in the Square outside the Parliament-House a Vast Concourse of affrighted people, and everywhere Foot-Soldiers (which have until this time been hid) standing to arms with Looks all Fierce and Resolute as to presage some Terrible Danger; and

* Bearing.

inquiring of one what the cause of these Alarums might be, he reply'd he is not SICCAR (which word in their Dialect signifies: certain or sure) but Dundee has climb'd the Crags to the Castle and plots with the Duke of Gordon (so 'tis rumour'd) to attack the Citie while the Batteries in the Castle do fire and a great bodie of Troops presently without the Citie do storm the Walls.

No sooner is he done telling me this, when the Doors of the Parliament-House are flung open and out comes the members of the Convention, the Whigs being receiv'd with Acclamation by the Populace (who hold 'em to be their Leaders and Protectors against the suppos'd Attack) but those of the opposite Partie with Threats and Curses. No Attack coming however, by and by the crowds go home, and finding Fletcher, I have a True Account of the Matter.

Dundee, (he says) goes down the Leith Wynd out of the Town, and riding with his Troop below the Castle looks up and espies Gordon who makes a Sign he would speak with him. Whereupon Dundee, his troop of 40 or 50 Horse waiting below, climbs up the Rocks to the Postern Gate and there confers with Gordon, perhaps, (says Fletcher) purposing to encourage him with the News his Royal Master has landed safe in Ireland.

—What, climb that Fearfull Precipice! I cry aghast;

—Even so, replys Fletcher, —for whatever charges his Enemies may prefer against him, they can never say Dundee lacks for Courage or a Cool Head. And the Duke of Hamilton, (continues he), perceiving some Advantage to his Partie here and a Stratagem to stir up the Populace against the Jacobites, caus'd it to be bruited about that Dundee and Gordon plotted to attack the Citie, &c.

3. After conferring with the Duke of Gordon awhile, Dundee goes on towards Linlithquo, which being

the road to Sterling, 'tis thought by the Convention, (says Fletcher) his Design may be to Surprize the Castle there, which commands the Pass of Communication between the North and South Parts of Scotland. The Convention ordered Major Buntin with 80 Horse to go after him: and the Earl of Mar, who is Governor of Sterling Castle, is gone to it by their Order, to secure it against any Surprize Attempt.

N.B. Fletcher thinks it unprobable Dundee intends anything against such a Strong Place with such a Paltrie Force as he presently hath. (Tho' as to what his True Purpose may be, that he cannot say.)

6.

‘ UPON THE FACE OF CAERKETTON ’

The Tilt-boat SOLAND,
March 20th, 1688/9.

NOW IS the World turn'd upside-down and I am sore troubled in mind, for I have been charg'd with the fulfilling of a further Dutie and that of so Weightie a Nature as quite to o'er-shadow my present businesse.

For now I am to follow after my Lord Dundee and by whatever means I may, learn what he purposes to do; which is as much above that which I was first requir'd by the Doctor to accomplish, as to catch a Tyger is above entrapping a Mouse. (Fletcher hath show'd to me a letter from the Doctor and countersigned by the Prince of Orange, granting unto Fletcher Power of Attorney as 'twere, to act as he thinks fit in the Doctor's room concerning the Matter in which I am presently engag'd. In a word, Fletcher is become Spymaster-Depute for the Doctor, who by reason he is 400 miles distant cannot know what is best should here be done in every Pass.) And all this is come about because Dundee hath untimely abandon'd the Convention for the reasons following, Viz:

1. There was a plot to murther him (tho' 'twas not fear for himself that moved him, I warrant, as con-

cern that he be prevented by Death from further serving his Liege).

2. The Convention being now resolv'd to choose the Prince of Orange, Dundee sees no purpose in further tarrying here.

I am to go by the Ferry from Leith to Bruntillian* then across Fife to the Firth or Aestuarium of the River Tay where is another Ferry (of but two miles) to the Citie of Dundee. Whence it is but a little way to Dudhope, the home of my Lord Dundee and where he is like to bide for the nonce. Here I am to spy upon Dundee, exercizing much Discretion, for all would go to pot should my purpose be discover'd. As to communication of Intelligence, I am not to use the Common Posts (says Fletcher) but at noon of a Monday to be at the Market Cross of Dundee when a pack-horse driver, by name Sandie Ogilvy, will meet with me, and who will be the means of exchanging letters between Fletcher and myself. (At our first meeting he will whistle the first stave of *Lilliburlero*, by which I will know him and am to make response by whistling the first stave of *Newcastle*.)

I own my heart something misgave me at this, for I recall'd 'twas Mr. Foe had first spoke to me of such traders, which caus'd me to inquire of myself, was that young man also privy to my Businesse? and was not there an exellent Maxim which holds that Too Many Cooks spoil the Pottage? I fear lest the Doctor's tongue may yet undo all.

But now, horresco referens,** I shall tell you of a Misadventure befell me this very morning (being the morning after Dundee was gone out of the Citie). All Work and no Play makes Jack a Dull Boy as the saying is, and being

* Burntisland.

** I shudder to relate.

sick of Edinburgh and its Alarums and the rough Westland Mobs (and to tell truth being something curious of viewing the country round about) I begg'd of Fletcher a Play-day from School as 'twere, the which he granted readily enow, as thinking it but prudent, I daresay, I should not follow too hot upon Dundee. And so found myself a-walking in the fields beyond the Burgh-Moor and by and by am come to Swanston, a hamlet at the foot of Pentland-Hills, a range of Mountains extending to the south and west of Edinburgh (and where at Rullion-Green these twenty and more years passed the Covenanting Westland men were beat by Generall Thomas Dalyell).

Here I resolv'd to heed the advise of the chirurgeons in London which had declar'd Hill Air to be very beneficiall for dispersing of the Ill Humours consequent upon my Sicknesse. And the day being calm and the sun a-shining (tho' 'twas passing cold) I step't out cheerfully enough upon the face of a steep mountain they call Caerketton. After about half-an-hour, being a little wearied I sate myself down upon a stone on a little level plain and was admiring the fine Prospect of the Castle and the Citie on its Ridge, and ships moving upon the face of the Firth, when I espied a man a-climbing of the slope below me. On his drawing nigh, I gave him good-day but never a word answer'd he, no not one, but continu'd in his Ascent, holding on a course that must cause him to pass by me very near; now could I see him plain, and an uncouth spectacle was he — very tall, and lean as a Skeletton, clad in common black, with a great old-fashion'd steeple-hat upon his head. I own I was vex'd by the fellow's surliness and something amaz'd to boot for thus far I had found the Scots (saving the wild Clydes-dale Hill-men) most punctilious as to all points of Civillity.

Just then, raising his head, the man look'd me plain in the face and of a sudden it was like as I had swallow'd a lump of Ice, for the look he gave me out of a pale countenance all sunk and hollow like a Skull was of such a Horrid Malignancie, I knew his purpose was to make an End of me.

Swiftly arising, I draw my small-sword, backing away as he rushes the last few yards to stand upon flat ground. He bares his blade, a long Spanish rapier, and advances towards me grinning like a Death's Head, with steps carefully plac'd as he were Agag which walked upon eggs. And in that moment my heart gives a great leap and I know I am sav'd, and I but keep a Cool Head, a Watchfull Eye, and a Steadie Hand.

For I perceive he places his feet in a Lozenge* Pattern, by which I know immediately he is but a Hired Bravo of Inferior Metal, school'd by some ancient rusty soldier which had learn'd his trade in the wars of Tilly and Wallenstein. For Swordplay of that time (with its curious Regiment nice and exact as any Dancing Master's, as: Ha! the Immortal Passado, &c.) is now-a-days quite given over. As I should know who have, for my Muse's sake, oft practis'd swordplay in Hyde Park of a morn with the lovely Mazarine or with Jane Middleton or certain other ladies of the Court, that I might instruct my Players in the Right Manner of Swordsmanship for their feign'd duellos upon the Stage (for which my Plays have been much admir'd).

He lunges, I parry with ease, reading his Intent in that Duck's-Foot Tread as plain as in any Book. Thrust, parry, riposte, 'tis like fencing with an Automaton. Now I have his measure and begin to press him; now he perceives his Error which is this – 'twould be but an Easy Matter to despatch a Meer Woman (for I doubt not that his Masters, some Desperate Band of Cavaliers of the stamp of the

* Diamond

Seal'd Knot, that had learn'd perchance of the Affaire in the tavern, have appris'd him of that circumstance) and she so obliging as to go a-walking in a Solitary Place. Now he begins to give back; truly is he hoist on his own petard for the fight now goes against him and there can be no Resolution of this Matter save in Death. Fear starts up in his eyes, he makes a desperate Thrust which I avoid meerly by swaying my body aside a little, causing him to stagger; as he strives to steadie himself I run him through the body. He falls upon his knees choking, a look of Amaze in his eyes, a great Jett of Blood gushes from his mouth and he dies.

For a little space after, I am assail'd by a Horrid Sicknesse and Swimming in my head, and am like to fall into a Swound.

But by and by these pass, and I make shift to retrace my steps to Edinburgh, leaving the corpse upon the bare hillside (for there was no place it could be conceal'd – neither tree nor bush nor wall, in all that open place). And making to return to my lodgings I am accosted by Fletcher (in a great Taking) as I enter into the Land-market, who salutes me with this unhappy Intelligence: Samuel is taken, and lock'd in the Tolbooth by the Magistrates who desire to question me. Therefore, (says Fletcher) 'tis is very necessarie I depart from Edinburgh instanter.

—But I cannot leave the lad behind, I cry.

—As to that you have no choice, returns Fletcher something brisk and grim, —for your Dutie requires you should. But be assur'd, (continues he) —I will see what can be done to help the Boy. As to your Portmanteau and Staff, I prevailed on the Magistrates to suffer I should keep 'em against your return, being but private Dunnage of no worth to any save yourself. And now, Mr. Johnson, we must haste to Leith, for the ferry waits upon the tide.

And so I departed from Edinburgh in a mighty Rush and Hurry, very sorrowful and in the Dumps on Samuel's account, and presently write this aboard the Tilt-boat on the Passage over.

—o-o-o—

Thus — in hurry and confusion, with the trauma of a killing and separation from her young protégé Samuel to prey on her mind, ends the first part of Aphra Behn's mission. With Dundee's sudden departure from Edinburgh, her role now undergoes a sea-change, from a passive to an active one, plunging her into protracted uncertainty, isolation and danger. Also, in following Dundee north, she will cross a psychological Rubicon. To the seventeenth century Lowlander or Englishman, the Scottish Highlands presented something of the aspect that Darkest Africa did to Victorian travellers — a trackless desolation of huge and horrible mountains inhabited by warlike and lawless savages, totally alien in culture, social organization, language and dress (the kilt was not then the interesting and admired garment it has become today, but the equivalent of the grass skirt), 'Terre inculte et sauvage', as the legend on a contemporary map puts it. To polite society of that era, 'The Highlanders' were a menacing anachronism, seen in something of the same light that inhabitants of the Roman Empire viewed the barbarian hordes beyond the Frontier.

PART TWO

P. Sleat
Egg I.
Kilmaroy
Loch Soil
Kilchamerin
L. Coich
INVERNE
Kinekie R.
Ard
Achaglin
Achagovonie
L. Garryf
Innercour
Ardoch
Monerig
Loch Murron
Loch Arkeg
Tirim
Ellan Finan
Loch Loch
Letyr Findlay
Kilmore
Castle Megarie
Loch Swyneord
LOCHABAR
Makomer
Kilman eval
Achinecich
Inch
Achanaßien
Torry Ch.
Donie
Fort william
Inner lochy
Balachenlas
Kean mor
Innet Coen
Anleurich
Pooldarig
L. Crevite
Reanloch
LORN
BRO
Dunstafag
Glenetyf
Kilbryd
Inisail R.
Iainnoch
Loch Aw
Barbeck
Inisthey
Anagra
Inver rary
Inyrlakan
Lochay
Achaßien
Loch Lomund
Luing I.
Scarba
The dangerous
of Cory

A T H O L E

Binachrow
Ness
M U R R A Y
Pluscardin
Midletoun
Dunawin
Glenkirk
Abyrnathy
Dulcimor
Ballachastel
Innernahalia
Inner Ishie
Rothymurkus
Clunie
Etrars
Spey R.
M A R
Glengardin
Castel toun
Loch Garry
Kilihona
A T H O L
Scarsoch
Blair
Gernich
Loch Timmel
Archagaul
Muylert
Lagan Ruit
Bal Eachan
Gart
Fay R.
Garntully
Bala
G A U R Y
Chap. of Glen Shir
Dunkeld
Loch Tay
Ballach
Almont R.
Ordy
Black
T R A T H E R N
Loch Erin
Newtoun
Inch Chafra
P E R T H
Compsie
Collas
Dundee
Errol
Drumond
Ardite
Abernethy
Tubbern
Yincarn
T E I T H
Dumblain
Lesly C.

7.

' IN PLAIN SIGHT OF THE GRAMPIAN MOUNTAINS '

Dunkeld,
April 18th, 1689.

I'VE DELAY'D to write in my Journall these three weeks and more by reason there hath occurr'd naught of import to record — that is untill these few days passed, when of a sudden great things are toward and Matters are like to move apace. And to pass from generalls to particulars, I shall here set down what hath transpired in the mean time.

Arriving in Dundee, a fair, well-built place rightly deserving of the name of Bonnie (signifying in their Dialect Fair or Handsome) by which 'tis known, I took lodgings in the Nether-Gate — the Retiring-Room as 'twere, from which I step't forth upon the Stage (of Forfar-Shire) to play my Part as the Cat i' the Fable which walk'd in boots. To explain: Fletcher hath charg'd me (upon our Parting at Leith), that I must be like to the Cat that watcheth at the Mouse-hole (Viz, Dudhope, the home of my Lord Dundee). Rather should he have said, the Mouse that watcheth at the Cat's Lair! I recall'd how in the Fable the Ogre had first changed himself into a Lion then into a Mouse, at which the Cat had pounc'd upon and kill'd him. But that was in the Fable; would that the Difficulties of this present Pass resolve themselves so easilie! (There be besides three other Matters which do trouble my Mind, Viz, 1. Having once essay'd to murther me, 'twould be meer fondness* to imagine that mine Enemies being check'd but the once, will now desist therefrom.

2. How did these Enemies, whoever they may be, come by Intelligence of my Design? I fear some Lapse of Discretion on the Doctor's part, to be the Cause.

3. I am much cast down at the thought that my young Friend Samuel, besides that he was a great Solace and Comfort for his Companionable and Engaging Manners, hath been sent back belike to that terrible Coal-Pit, and his estate now more wretched and miserable than heretofore, and that were possible).

I soon made shift to espy out Dudhope, but there being nothing other I could do to further my Cause, and my Lord Dundee by common report biding quietly at home, I thought it prudent not to attempt anything more at this time. By the way, my Lord Dundee is much respected (or fear'd?) here, for his stern un-partial Justice when Provost, for all that he hath been declar'd a Traitor, and his Authoritie be now defunct.

Upon my second meeting with Sandie Ogilvy (a merry loquacious fellow with a cast to his eye and which clokes a sharp Wit beneath a Buffoon's Semblance), he gives me a letter from Fletcher advising me that Dundee's Commission from King James had been despatch'd from Ireland but had misluck'd and fall'n into the hands of the Convention together with letters to Dundee and Balcarres writ by Melfort; whereat the Convention is mighty enrag'd, for Melfort says their army is to be pay'd for by the Estates of the present Lords of the Convention who are moreover to become Hewers of Wood and Drawers of Water. In

* Foolishness.

consequence whereof 100 of Leven's and 100 Scots Dragoons under Sir Thos. Livingston have been despatch'd to apprehend Balcarres and Dundee respectively. Also in Fletcher's letter: the Prince of Orange hath been proclaim'd King in Edinburgh. And post scriptum – this Request: that should Dundee quit Dudhope, I am to follow in pursuit or otherwise act as Sandie shall advize. (Which doth bring me near unto Despair, for I begin to think that I shall never be quit of this Businesse.)

Yesterday, Sandie seeks me out in my lodgings to inform me of this following Intelligence (which he hath come by through the gossip of a soldier's Jade): that Col. William Livingston, (a kinsman of Sir Thomas), and the Scots Dragoons by reason they were of Dundee's old regiment and his Fellow-Campaigners, presently desire to enter into the Service of my Lord Dundee.

But before the Regiment could effect a meeting with Dundee, that Bird hath flown; this very morning among a great concourse from the Town, I watch'd with Sandie, my Lord Dundee in brave scarlet and before his Troop, unfurl the Royal Banner on the Dundee Law, then ride off to the northwards. At which sight my heart did pain me sore for my Naturall Inclination was to cast my lot with Dundee and follow his gallant little Band. (Which will never come to pass however sore my heart, for that particular private Battle hath been fought already and the Issue decided, as you know.)

And after witnessing my Lord Dundee's departure I made haste to inform Fletcher of it in a letter which I gave into Sandie's keeping, and so rode incontinent* to Dunkeld (which Sandie advises may be nearer to Dundee's Itinerary, and where Sandie will make shift to meet with

* Without delay.

me, a distance of 30 Scotch Miles westwards and something northwards from the Town of Dundee). At which place I arriv'd but these two hours passed, it then being seven o' clock in the evening, and am presently lodg'd and my nag stabled.

As to Dunkeld (or Dunkell as some call it) which is in the Sherrifdom of Perth, on the north bank of Tay and surrounded by pleasant Woods, 'tis but a mean place scarce more than a Village tho' formerlie much larger, and now sunk in the full perfection of Decaye tho' 'tis here thought of almost as a Metropolis, being a chief Market-Town of the Highlands and the Bishop's Seat. The Ruins of the Cathedral Church (a remaining part whereof is used for worship) are yet to be seen, but that which chiefly adorns Dunkeld are the Stately Buildings lately erected by the Marquess of Athole. Tho' Dunkeld is accounted a Town of the Highlands 'tis not truly so, for tho' in plain sight of the Grampian Mountains, the country round about is in part low lying and fertile (or rather could be made so if the inhabitants were more industrious), something broken with hills and woods.

In my letter to Fletcher I advis'd that he urge the Convention to send Generall MacKay northwards, for it is my belief (or rather I am persuaded by Sandie Ogilvy to believe) that in spite of the mis-carrying of his Commission, Dundee purposes to raise the Clans to fight for King James.

P.S. And so I wait here at the EDGE (as 'twere), in expectation of News from Sandie, and look upon these Horrible Mountains amongst which my Fancie depicts my Lord Dundee a-riding and a-riding, and a terrible savage Host a-gathering till the time come when they shall be let slip and the land filled with

Blood and Slaughter. And, God help me, there is a part of me would rejoyce thereat.

—o-o-o—

It would seem that, following Aphra Behn's advice, Fletcher did persuade the Convention to send MacKay north; for we find the Commander-in-Chief of the Williamite forces in Scotland arriving in Dundee about the 28th of April. There followed a complicated game of cat-and-mouse around the eastern fringes of the Grampian mountains with Dundee the Lowlander displaying infinitely more flair and initiative in this sort of manoeuvring than his old fellow-campaigner MacKay — a Highlander born and bred.

Meanwhile, through a combination of charm, tact, patience and appeal on a personal level, Dundee's efforts to win over the clans were proving markedly more successful than MacKay's. (For details see Appendix: John Graham of Claverhouse.) In that stark phrase, 'at the EDGE', Aphra Behn tellingly conveys the foreboding and sense of 'alienness' which the Highlands and their inhabitants aroused in the Southerner.

8.
‘ BEYOND THE EDGE ’

Fortingall,
12th May, 1689.

TWO SENNIGHTS* did pass and no word from Sandie, then a travelling tinker sought me out privily and that gave me a Billet with the place and time of an Assignation writ therein. And the appointed day being come, off I set on foot from Dunkeld, taking passage across Tay (which here flows very broad and deep) by a ferry-boat of which severall are kept mighty busy plying constantly betwixt the north and the south shores.

In consideration of the traffic engender'd by Dunkeld, I wonder they have neglected to build a bridge which would vastly increase the Commerce of the place to the great Profitt of the inhabitants; but I've observ'd 'tis not in the Nature of the people in this Part of Scotland to labour above what is absolutely Necessarie, even when to do so must benefit 'em greatly. But this by the way.

Arriving at the Confluence of Tay with Bran, a stream of no great width to be sure, but mighty swift and strong, I climb'd along above the bank of this latter river till by and by I am come to a narrow gorge below a hill (which place Sandie had describ'd exactlie in his Billet, and which I'd already made shift to mark out, to the end that our meeting together should not miscarry). Here the stream

* A fortnight (two 'seven-nights')

plunges over a steep Precipice to go roaring and tumbling into a Fearfull Chasm, and with such force as to cause the very ground to tremble.

I had not waited above an hour at this Ghastly Spot when I heard someone a-whistling of *Lilliburlero* a little way off. Smiling to myself (for 'tho I was in plain sight, Sandie must needs play the Spy showing ev'ry nice attention to Proper Usage as he were an Ambassador at the Court of the Grand Cham of Tartary or some such), I gave back *Newcastle,* upon which out step't Sandie from behind an alder-tree. On my inquiring of him what were the News, he looks all about him, his wall-eye a-rolling, as to be certain we were indeed alone, then coming close inclines his mouth towards my ear (tho' what with the Roaring of the Linn no one could have heard us above a yard's distance), and tells me Dundee hath summoned the Clans to meet with him.

At which Intelligence my heart gives a great Bound, for this is War!

—And where and when is this Meeting to be? I ask.

—Houts, Sir, fou' fa' me and I ken, (replys he). —But dinna fash yersel, Sir; be ye here twa days on at echt o' the Nock in the morn, and I'se hae speired thon oot. (By which he signified he did not know, but not to vex myself, for and I return at eight o' clock two days hence he'd have discovered the Answer.)

And so I bad tryst* for Sandie but something early (being mighty wakeful in the night on account of my Eagerness to learn what were his News) which was my Salvation I daresay, for soon after I was come to the Place, I heard two Reports as they might be Pistol-shots, from some distance ahead, and in a little space Sandie breaks from a coppice of birch-trees and comes a-running to

* Waited at the appointed time and place.

where I stand, and commands me that I follow after him in climbing down the rocks above the Linn. I look over that Horrible Cliff at the Foaming Tumult far below and am terrify'd.

—'Tis Death to venture there! I cry.

—'Tis Death tae bide here, (returns he) —but gae yeir ain Gait, and ye will; and with that begins to clamber down that Hideous Wall. Near swounding with Terror, and my heart in my mouth as the saying is, I am constrain'd to follow and with Infinite Care begin to climb after Sandie, placing my hands and feet where I observe he places his, in cracks and ledges so narrow and so slick with the Spray from the Cataract, I am convinc'd I must slip and so fall. But by and by, coming level with a great out-jutting Rock, Sandie crawls beneath it and I do likewise to find we are on a platform with the Rock o'er-hanging us as to form a shelter'd Recess, secure from Observation from above.

For a moment I am fill'd with Thankfulness, both on account of being spared awhile from the Horror of our Descent, and for being safe for a space from our Enemies. Then I observe that Sandie is deadly pale, his face cover'd in a sheen of sweat, and that Blood issues from his side in great slow Drops.

—Why Sandie — you're hurt! I cry.

—Nay Sir, I'm dead, replys he. —Now wheesht ye and harken weel for I hanna muckle time.

Then he relates to me (I placing my ear close on account of the Thunder of the Falls and his voice being so low) his Intelligence under these severall Heads as following:

1. The clans are to meet with Dundee on the 18th of May.

2. Dundee (who receives Intelligence through his Lady in Glen Ogilvy) having raided in a single night both

Dunkeld and Perth for specie and supplies, is presently in Angus a-gathering of money and followers, and hopes to join with the Scots Dragoons quarter'd in Dundee and which have privily made known their wish to serve under their old Commander. (Touching which aforesaid Raid, it had needs been manag'd exceeding stealthy for I'd heard no Bruit thereof.)

3. Generall MacKay (who until of late hath been in Ignorance that Dundee is in the Lowlands) is presently in Inverness.

4. Tho' the time of the Clans' Assembling is known, the place is not; Sandie thinks it may be in Lochaber (which is in the Western Highlands) by reason that he knows Dundee hath corresponded much with Sir Ewen Cameron of Lochiel, whose Territory is in that Part.

—Mackay and the Convention must be warn'd! I broke out. —And there's but little time; Dundee meets with the Clans on the 18th you say, and tomorrow is the 13th; what's to do?

—Here's whit ye maun dae, Sir, says Sandie (in a voice scarce more than a whisper), —Dundee willna tak the High Road tae Lochaber by Blair o' Athole and the Pass of Drumochter, for yon is like tae be watchit by MacKay's sodgers; belike he'll gang stracht across Scotland by Rannach, then nor' atween Ben Alder and Ben Nevis tae Spean whilk is in Lochaber. So ye maun watch and bide for Dundee at a spot on his Line o' March, then follow efter him tae the Gatherin'-place o' the Clans.

—'Tis Impossible, I exclaim, in a kind of Extasy of Despair (thinking of that Howling Wilderness of Mountains) for I had no knowledge of the Countrie, nor of the

Ways by which it might be travers'd, nor of its Peoples (of whose Language I was moreover utterlie ignorant).

—Haud up, Sir, (returns Sandie), —ye maun pit a stoot Hert til a Stae Brae.

And of a sudden I am fill'd with Shame that a man so near to Death should yet remain so compos'd, while I should suffer my Concern thus to manifest itself. And now Sandie explains to me how there be only so many Ways through the Mountains, Viz, by the Valleys (or Glens as they call 'em) of the Lochs and Rivers, so that what at first sight seems an un-passable Tangle of Hills is in truth travers'd by a number of deep Troughs (in the room of Roads as 'twere) by a knowledge of which a traveller will find a Sure Passage thorough the Highlands.

By the eastern end of the Loch call'd Rannach, Sandie now said, was a tall Mountain, Schehallion, in form like to a Sugar-loaf, from the top of which and the day were clear, I might see all the Countrie through which Dundee must pass (that is, should Sandie be aright in his Surmise). I then ask'd how distant the Mountain was and how I should travel thither, to which Sandie made reply 'twas 30 miles north-westwards from Dunkeld; and he gave me exact directions how I should reach it, by way of a Town nam'd Fortingall. Here I should pass the night at the house of one Colin Du, that is Black Colin, a tacksman to Campbell of Glenlyon (a tacksman in Highland Society signifying a Lessee of a Superior Kind). Once in Glen-Lyon I may count myself safe (Sandie assur'd me), Clan Campbell being strong for the Orange Party.

Sandie now urg'd me that I possess myself of his Satchel wherein he said, were severall Useful and Necessarie Articles, for I must in no wise return to Dunkeld (where were my nag, my portmanteau, my money in Specie and in Promissory Notes, and my Measuring Staff; tho' by God's Mercie not my Journall which, together with a

Writing-compact, I keep always on my Person) for 'twas sure to be watched by our Enemies, one of whose number had slain him. And he told me how, after leaving his pack-train with a certain trustworthie person, he had set out for the Trysting-place (but by a different road from mine) and had fall'n into an Ambuscade, two fellows in Lowland Habit and with guns in their hands of a sudden rising from behind a Rock at a little distance from the path and shooting at him; one ball miss'd but t'other struck him in the side. But, knowing the Nature of the Countrie, Sandie had contriv'd to win clear of his Assailants and lose 'em, but not before he had observ'd at a greater distance, a third man very tall and thin and muffl'd in a dark cloke appear from among trees, and who seem'd from his gestures to be urging the others to pursuit. As to who they might be, saving that they were friends to King James which had learn'd of my Design (or hired by such), he could make no guess.

Sandie being now grown very weak, entreated of me that I take his Hand in mine and to say with him the Words of the Lord's Prayer, which service I perform'd very willingly (tho' in a voice something broken); but we had scarce utter'd Thy Kingdom Come, when he gave a Sigh, his head roll'd upon one side, and his Spirit departed from him.

Sandie's Death, and the Manner of it, and the Desparate Pass in which of a sudden I now found myself, did put me in a kind of Numb Stupor of Horror and Miserie compounded. How long I sate there beside poor Sandie's corpse I have no reckoning, but it must have been a not inconsiderable space, for Sandie's hand was cold when I unclasp'd mine from it, and I was passing chill'd and stiff. Then I bethought me 'twas no time to show Cowardlie Weaknesse, and that for Sandie's sake (if for none other) which had died for the Cause I serv'd and had shown such

Exemplarie Courage and Dutifulness before his Passing, I must bestir myself.

Mine Enemies I thought would by this time belike be gone, perhaps concluding that (on account of they had not found his bodie tho' knowing him to be sore wounded) he had essay'd to cross the stream to escape 'em but had been carry'd over the Linn. I had Sufficiency of Wit remaining to know that the more I delay'd to climb that Terrible Precipice, the less stomach I would have for the task, so slinging Sandie's Satchel around my shoulder, I edg'd myself out onto the Cliff and began to ascend. Perhaps it was a new-found Anger against mine Enemies which, driving out Fear nerv'd me for the Ascent; but I climb'd steadily and surely without once dwelling on the Perils of my Situation, and in a little space was arriv'd at the top and clamb'ring over the edge stood safe upon Level Ground once more.

Looking around and being satisfy'd I was not observ'd, I set off at a brisk pace along the bank of Bran (if it can properly be called a bank that stands so high above the stream). By and by the Valley begins to be less steep and the Angle of its inclosing slopes to decline, so that soon I am able to walk near to the water's edge. And after about five miles I am come to the meeting of Bran and a lesser stream, which river I follow northwards over lumpy grass and heather-bushes with a high steep Ridge on one side and broken hills upon the other.

In a few miles more, having thus far espied not another soul in the Way, I am come to the Head-waters of this stream, with a low Pass before me (just such as Sandie had describ'd), and being gone thorough this Pass, am content to sit me down and rest awhile. Before me the ground drop't down to the broad valley of Tay, with the Town of Aberfeldy close by the River on the hither side, and beyond the river a Row of Dark Mountains which my

Fancie likens to the Vanguard of an Enemie Host. And now I mind me of Sandie's Satchel and opening it discover the following:

1. A fine Perspective Glasse.*
2. A bag of Money, mostly silver and copper but has 3 Guineas besides.
3. A small Mariner's Compass.
4. A Map.
5. A Razor.

I made triall of the Perspective and was amaz'd and delighted on looking through it at the Town, to see the Houses and People spring out sharp and clear, as I might be looking upon a Painted Picture. Then, spreading the Map upon a stone, there was the Countrie exactlie as Sandie had depicted it with those Passages thorough the Mountains he had spoke of. Then of a sudden I am put in mind by these Articles (by which, saving the Razor, my Task will be made infinitely the easier) of poor Sandie a-lying in that Dreadfull Place, and burst into Tears; and I vow to myself that when all this Businesse shall be done, I'll return and give his Bones Christian Buriall.

At last, something calm'd, I descended the Incline before me and so came to the Town of Aberfeldy, which is in truth but a dirty Village, tho' no doubt accounted here a Vast Metropolis by reason a few houses of the better sort have Glasse in their windows and the Street is in a manner pav'd by having round River-stones set end-wise into the road-bed. Here, as in Dunkeld, the townsfolk wear the Lowland Garb and for the most part speak English as readily as Irish.** After fortifying myself at a tap-house with some indifferent collops and a mug of Aqua

* Telescope.

** Gaelic

Vitae (or Uiskeyva as they call it and which they drink as freely as Ale) I press'd on to the Ferry where (belike perceiving I was a Foreigner and ignorant of the Tolls) the ferryman refus'd to carry me over Tay for under two shillings! There being no help for it I pay'd him, tho' mighty sullen, and was set down on the farther bank by a little scatter of filthie huts Viz, the Town of Weem. (Here also at a little distance is a strong Keep call'd Castle Mingis.)

Keeping the broad and level valley of Tay on my left hand, I set my face to the westwards and following a pretty good path, arriv'd in but a few miles at the meeting of Tay and Lyon. Here I bade farewell to Tay, and keeping Lyon on my left hand as Sandie had directed me, after I had waded across a considerable brook flowing into Lyon from the north, enter'd into Glen-Lyon.

And now a Chill, as 'twere, descended on my Spirits, and I thought that now truly I was indeed beyond the EDGE, for on either hand the Mountains rose up Dark and Horrible, and in the distance ahead of me rising to such a Prodigious Height and being all a-speckl'd by Snow as did put me in mind of the Alps.

Such a Gloomie Desert you'd think would be uninhabited but 'twas not so, for I pass'd severall dwellings, the vilest habitations imaginable rudely fashion'd from un-mortar'd stones, and with roofs of turfs secured against the winter tempests by nets of ropes a-weighted with rocks. And about these hovels, fowls and goats and goat-like sheep a-foraging for such scantie sustenance as they could find, also little black kine no bigger than mastiffs tott'ring and staggering as they pastur'd, so weak were they after their winter Fasting. Nor were the people in much better case it seem'd to me than their Bestial*

* Livestock.

(belike from the same Cause) appearing hollow-fac'd and thin as Skelletons as they laboured in their stony Gardens (which to call fields would be much as to call Highgate-Hill a Loftie Mountain). Yet (lest I appear too censurious) I must allow that these beggarly-looking folk lack nothing for Good Manners for they did greet me very civilly as I passed 'em by. Also their Clothes, which in the men is a great plaid chequer'd in many colours and belted around the waist, seem very cunningly and curiously woven.

At last, between 5 and 6 o' clock at night (as near as I could tell by the Sun which was presently declining betwixt the valley walls directlie to my fore) having travell'd about twenty-five miles without great weariness, I am come to Fortingall, a meer row of cabins in no wise distinguishable from the others I had observ'd in this valley; the presence of a Church however, suffers the inhabitants to esteem their settlement a Place of Consequence. On my inquiring as to which was the house of Colin Du, I am directed to his hut, it standing something apart from the others, and am greeted by a pockmark'd man of middle height, without shoes, stockings or breeches, in a short coat, with a shirt not much longer to hide his Nakednesse.

I tell him I am come from Sandie and announce my melancholie News, whereat he makes the sign of the Cross and mutters some Popish Incantation. Then, bowing to me very civill, he invites me inside his Dwelling, which is very long but without ceiling or any partition, some Cattle at one end and at the other the Familie consisting of his wife, two daughters in their 'teen years, and three servants. In the midst, dividing the domain of the Beasts from that of the Humans, a fire of Peats smold'ring, the smoak whereof being suffer'd to escape by a hole in the roof.

Yet in despite of all this Filth and Povertie, the Civillity display'd by my host (which by the way speaks English exellently well, and with little of the Scottish Dialect to marr it) is impeccable and would put to shame the Manners of many of our English Squires, nay of some of our Nobilitie to boot; also, what was to me a great wonder, a shelf of Books among them Sir Thos. Urquart's translation of Rabelais and the Verses of Wm. Drummond of Hawthornden. While supper was a-readying, the Tacksman took me to the Churchyard to see a great Marvell and to hear of a greater, for here is a vast and ancient Yew-tree (the girth whereof I reckon to be above fiftie feet) which he declar'd was already very old when Pontius Pilate was born here! Which, tho' a mighty Engaging Tale is Nonsensicall, for the Conquest of Britain was not begun until the time of Claudius Caesar, ten years after the Death and Resurrection of Our Lord, nor was the Invasion of Scotland by Agricola put in hand for a further forty years. But this by the way.

At Supper, which was a wretched repast of Cow's Blood boil'd to a Cake, with a little milk and a pinch of oatmeal (which is very generall in the Highlands in the Spring, when their winter stores begin to fail) it came on to rain, and the water coming through the roof and mingling with the Soot on the rafters did splash on the floor like great drops of Ink. What with the smarting of my eyes from the Peat-smoak, the singing of my head from the strong Punch (great Draughts of which I was constrain'd to drink with the rest of the Companie, for fear of appearing un-mannerly), the biting of Vermin and the constant dripping of Water, I found Sleep to be impossible, when I was eventually suffer'd to go to bed. And so, by the light of a Candle (curiously made from the pitchy core of a Pine-tree) I writ up my Journall compleat to this present time.

9.

' A BLEAK AND GHASTLIE WILDERNESSE '

Glen-Spean,
16th May, 1689.

THE MORNING FOLLOWING (that being the 13th day of May), my host himself offer'd to conduct me to the Mountain Schehallion, which kindnesse I was verie willing to accept, both by reason that his Companie would lighten the Journey thither somewhat, also I had hopes he might furnish me with Useful Intelligence touching the Affections of the Clans. After our breaking our fast with oat-bread dip't in milk, we set off to the eastwards along Glen-Lyon the sun a-rising in our faces, mounted on shaggy little horses scarce bigger than a large dog, that our feet near trailed upon the ground. My host, both for Convenience in Riding and for Decencie as going abroad, had put on the Trews which is a close-fitting Trowsers in a cloth of chequer'd pattern cut on the cross, these being worn by Highland Gentrie in preference to the Plaid, they generallie travelling a-horseback.

Being come to the stream at the entrance to Glen-Lyon (the same which I'd crossed the day before), we turned our faces to the North and keeping the stream on our right hand press'd on through a heatherie Valley. As we travell'd, the Tacksman advis'd me that all this Countrie betwixt the Lochs of Tay and Rannach and as far to the westwards almost as Loch Awe, is call'd Braid-Alban, being a Territorie of the strong and increasing Clan Campbell which hath two Principall Divisions, Viz, Braid-Alban whose chief is Sir John Campbell, a verie wise and cunning man, who was made Earl by King Charles II but eight years passed and is now staunch for the House of Orange; Argyll, being the South-Western Highlands betwixt the Firths of Lorn and Clyde with all the Coasts and Islands thereof and whose Chief stands high in William's favour. Beyond Braid-Alban to the northwards (he continu'd) was the Countrie of Athole whose Chief (in imitation of the Ostrich!) was presently a-taking of the Waters in Bath, and had, at Generall MacKay's bidding, urg'd his son Lord John Murray (a verie proud and passionate man) to persuade the men of Athole in his room that they join not with my Lord Dundee. However 'tis not certain he'll succeed, (said Colin Du), the Atholemen being generallie verie strong for King James in their hearts. Northwards again from Athole are the Countries of Badenoch and Moray; here, the Chiefs of Clan MacPherson and Clan MacIntosh have declar'd neither for King James nor King William ('tis Colin call'd him King; for myself he remains the Prince of Orange). In conclusion, to the westwards of Athole (that is, north-westwards from Braid-Alban), the Clans of the Countries of Arisaig and Lochaber are thought to be generallie of the Jacobite Partie, Viz, Camerons of Lochiel, Stewarts of Appin, MacLeans of Duart and Morven, MacNeils of Barra, MacLeods of Raasay, and MacDonalds of Moydart and the Isles, of Glen-Garry, of Glen-Coe and of Keppoch. (The Clans of the Northern Highlands, Rosses, Sinclairs, &c., as being so remote from any possible Theatre of War, were not like to join one side or t'other Colin said.) In a word: the South and South-Western Highlands are for the House of

Orange; the Western Highlands are for King James; the Middle Highlands are as yet for neither Partie.

On my asking, and it came to War which side would have the more advantage? he reply'd he thought the Jacobite Clans on account of they were headed by Sir Ewen Cameron, and he went on to tell me of this Great man: how he had slain the last Wolf in Scotland; how with but 35 men he had attack'd Generall Monck's English force of 300 at Inverlochy slaying 138 of them, and himself biting out an Englishman's throat; how he had compell'd Monck to a Treatie, and at the Restoration was presented by him to King Charles II. And tho' now advanc'd in years is yet hale and strong and fam'd throughout the Highlands for his great Deeds. (Colin allows however that the Jacobite Clans are mov'd not so much by Loyaltie to the House of Stewart as hatred of Clan Campbell which they look on as their Naturall Enemie.)

By this time we are come within plain sight of the Mountain (which is exceeding high, tho' not so much resembling a Sugar-loaf as I had suppos'd it must, on account peradventure of our approaching it something from the south-east for here the Mountain extends itself in a vast Promontorie). At a point where the stream began to trend to the westwards we arriv'd at a cottage outside which a child was squatting (stark-naked despite it being cold) in the performance of that Dutie to which Nature compels us all but which most of us make shift to do privilie. Here dwelt a bowman of Colin's (a bowman being what we would call a leaseholder but which takes stock from his superior and shares with him the increase thereof).

After he had introduc'd me to the bowman's wife (her goodman being on the hill), Colin advis'd me I should bide here until my Purpose be accomplish'd. (By which I am persuaded to believe he knows something of my Businesse, peradventure serving in the same Cause as myself, and belike employ'd by Fletcher.) He then presented me with three verie necessarie Articles: a Plaid to serve both as cloke against the weather and blankett at night; a bag of Oatmeal (which he says being mix't with water will provide a Sustaining Food, and indeed I need no other); a tin Pannikin, to serve as cup, platter, or basin as requir'd. And went on to say that I may with perfect Securitie confide in him any Intelligence I wish to be convey'd (which confirms me in my Suspicion he is privy to my Design). Whereupon he took his leave of me; and here I did make a most Grievous Error, seeking to press on him a little Money in recompense for his Hospitalitie.

—You will pardon me if I speak plain, Mr. Johnson, said he, (mighty offended) —but there is a thing you would never do and that is to offer your dirtie Monie to a Hieland shentleman.

Much abash'd I apologiz'd as handsomelie as I might, pleading Ignorance as to the Customs of the Countrie, and my Mortification being so plain, he is constrain'd to repent a little and gives me his Hand (tho' something stiff, to be sure). And so, leading my nag by the bridle, rides off back the way we have come.

After partaking of a little oatmeal gruel (which they call Broase) the goodwife brings me in a horn cup, I depart from the cottage (which to liken to a Pigsty would be compliment indeed) and begin to climb the Mountain by the Ridge or Promontorie I spake of and find it not so Arduous as I'd fear'd, tho' something marshie at the start, and the Heather-bushes troublesome to my feet. By and by, as I approach nearer to the Summit, the grass and heather give room to Loose Stones (in places cover'd by Snow), verie slipp'ry to walk upon and causing me a good deal of Scrambling and Puffing before I stand upon the Top.

Being so high above the Ground, the Prospect upon ev'rie side seems of an Infinit Extent, a Sea of Hills as 'twere, the Foamie Billows whereof are the snow-cover'd Mountain-tops. Looking on Sandie's Map, I am able after a little triall to mark certain places shown therein, as: the Lochs of Tummell and Rannach lying directlie to the North of the Mountain and on my right and left hands respectively; a verie Lofty Mountain rising many miles to the North-west and which is belike Ben Alder which Sandie spake of; Westwards from Loch Rannach, a dreary Desart of low broken ground and beyond it the Mouth of a Monstrous Valley, around which Gloomie Mountains stand thick as Tombstones in a Churche-yard. With my Perspective Glasse I view by degrees the entire Valley of the afore-mention'd Lochs, by which Passage peradventure Dundee will come, but espy naught save Bestial a-feeding and folk like moving Dots around the Clachans (which is what we would call Hamlets).

It was passing cold upon the Mountain-top and I became mighty chill'd, but there was no remedie for that, my Dutie constraining me to keep watch until it should fall dark. The sun being gone down, I came down the Mountain, finding something to my surprise that 'twas more tiresome to descend than to go up, and by and by, after making severall false casts (it now being grown quite dark) I made my way to the stream and so back to the bowman's Cottage. Here I found the bowman to be so affected by Strong Waters as to be scarce sensible of my presence, and presently falls into a Stupor. The children being abed, the goodwife set meat and drink before me and sat herself beside me while I did eat, which Exercise I necessarilie perform'd in Silence, having as much Irish* as she had English, which is to say none at all. At first I imagin'd

* Gaelic

'twas meer Civillitie which compell'd her to this Dutie, but by and by, she pressing her Bodie 'gainst mine, sighing and putting her Head upon my shoulder, 'twas plain she was mov'd by another Cause altogether, she thinking me to be a Man and a handsome one to boot — for I've been prais'd for my Looks times enough to know I can count 'em among my Assets. (I hope you will excuse this Observation; 'twas not made from Vanitie, but meerly to explain the Woman's interest in my Person.)

Tho' I was fain to smile, 'twas in truth no Jesting Matter, for and she were to discover my true Sex, the Securitie of my Task would be put in Jeopardie, for (unless she differ'd from the rest of her Sex) 'twas un-conceivable she'd not delight to gossip of her Discoverie. I suffer'd her to kiss and clip* me (for to do less were scarce mannerlie; and besides 'twas no sore Penance to endure, she being a mighty pretty woman and passionate to boot), the while partaking liberallie of Aqua Vitae to the end I might be furnish'd with Excuse for failing in a Lover's Part (for Drink in excess, as Shakespear doth confirm, increases Desire while preventing Performance; indeed I felt sorry for the poor woman, on account of my being such an un-servicable Man to her — as you will understand and you have read my poem, the Disappointment). By and by, imagining me to be dead drunk, (which indeed I was!) she suffer'd me (tho' mighty reluctantly) to go to bed, and so for a second night I retir'd with my Head a-singing.

The next day (which was the 14th) differ'd in no essentials from the previous, Viz, I climb'd the Mountain, watch'd for Dundee in vain, became exceeding chill'd, descended the Mountain, disappointed the Hopes of my would-be Paramour, and so went to bed drunk. But on the 15th, a little after sunrise, I did see from the Moun-

* Embrace

tain-top a little twinkling point of light far away to the Eastwards, then as by degrees the Darknesse vanish't from the Valley below me, I espied more and yet more flashes. And looking towards that Part through my Perspective Glasse I see like Beads on a Rosarie, a row of glitt'ring specks a-dipping up and down by Tummel-side; 'tis Dundee! of that I have no doubt.

Hastening down the Mountain as fast as may be, I collect my Plaid and Bag of Meal from the bowman's cottage. The goodwife accompanying me a little upon my way, we take a silent Farewell of each other, she looking upon me with Eyes fill'd with Longing, and kisses me right wantonly. (Tho' and she had known I was but a feign'd Man, she had never fallen in love I daresay, for that were to be enamour'd of a Chimeera,* as 'twere). Setting my face to the North with the Mountain to my left hand, I came thorough a Pass and in something over an hour arriv'd at the banks of the Tummel River where it issueth from its Loch. The river here being broad and deep and my having no leisure to seek out the Ferrie, I prevail'd upon an old man whom I espied a-setting of his nets, to carry me over in his Skiff; the which he did verie willingly and would take no payment.

Hiding myself in a Grove of little stunted Ash-trees (which in Scotland they call Rowans) overlooking a Path which did run beside the river, I crouch'd me down to wait. But I was not long at that businesse when I heard the clop of horses' Feet and the jingling of Bridle-bits and here is Dundee and his Troop a-riding by me so close I could with ease have cast a Pebble 'mongst 'em. Verie brave and gay they appear at first sight, array'd in shining Back-and-breasts, bright Coats, Beaver Hats with Plumes a-nodding and glitt'ring Helmets. Then I perceive by the

* A fabulous monster; metaphorically and impossible fancy.

stumbling Gait of their Mounts, the drawn unshav'n faces of the Riders, and the rust-speckles on the Armour that perforce they've ridden long and hard, belike with but little pause for Bait.* Yet for all their manifest Fatigue, they carry themselves proudlie and with Spirits high, none more so than my Lord Dundee which turning in the saddle, with a cheerful Countenance calls on 'em to close up Ranks, chiding 'em (in jest) for Laggards and says their Granddams would make better time. Whereat there's Laughter (tho' something wearie to be sure) and a Shaking of Heads as they move closer together; then are they passed. Truly, and I were a man, I'd follow such a Leader to the Ends of the Earth.

For a little space after their Rearguard was gone out of sight I waited in my Hiding-place, then set out to follow. 'twas not possible of course to keep their Pace, but there was no fear of losing 'em what with the marks of the horses' Feet upon the Road and the Dung thereof. By and by I am come to Loch Rannach side, the path following the North Shore, all this part easie Travelling, for 'tis level by the Water and the path pretty good save where Streams descending from the Slopes above do cross it where they come into the Loch. And now, looking across the Loch I see Schehallion, resembling a vast Sugar-loaf even as Sandie had said; and on the farther shore a mighty Forest, cov'ring all the sides of the Mountains to perhaps two-thirds of their height.

However, once passed the Western end of the Loch of Rannach, all Ease of Journeying is left behind, for here the path falters and vanishes as you enter into a Bleak and Ghastlie Wildernesse, where is no living thing to be seen save Crows and Eagles. To the Southwards extends that low Desert Place I espied from the Top of Schehallion,

* Refreshment (for either horses or men) taken on a journey

all a-pitted with Black Ponds of standing water, with here and there Dead Trees as gaunt and pale as Skelletons; to North and West a Waste of Mountains Bare and Frightfull, all ring'd around a broken hollow Land into which I must now pass, for I see by the marks upon the ground that Dundee's Troop have gone this way.

The Horror of this next part of my Journey I cannot well describe. The land, rising by Degrees, becomes more and more expos'd and in consequence the colder, so as 'twere you ascend back into Winter. Here, are the Gulleys fill'd with Snow-water running fast and deep, the earth itself a Frozen Crust that yieldeth ever and again, that your legs plunge into the Bog beneath. Of a sudden, a cold Mist descending from the Hollows high up in the Mountains did put me in a great Terror of losing the Way. Before the mist closes round me however, I mark my direction (which is to the North-westwards) with the aid of my Mariner's Compass, and hold to that Poynt, tho' soon I can see naught for mist, that swirls about me like to an Icey Smoak.

By and by, the mist dispersing, I find to my unspeakable Joy I am still in the Way, by this Melancholie Proof: here is a poor horse which having broke thorough the frozen ground to stick fast in the Slough beneath, hath been shot and left behind. These Gloomie Sign-posts continuing, I press on, stumbling from Wearinesse, chill'd and shiv'ring, and much troubl'd in Spirit by Doubts and Fears touching the carrying out of my Design. At last, as darknesse begins to spread, the ground becomes level then descends, the Mountains now drawing in close on either hand, and now below me to my fore I see the Head of a Loch, all hemm'd in with steep high Slopes, and by the water's edge a distant huddle of Horses and Men (some wrapp'd in blanketts), stands of Arms and the smoak of Camp-fires. I was by this time so fatigu'd, and moreover confus'd in my Mind, as to be pretty nigh insensible of the Necessitie to take Precautions 'gainst being observ'd. But so belike were they, for they had no Vedettes posted that I could see. Having no stomach for food, I wrapp'd myself in my Plaid (which I found to be wonderfullie proof 'gainst cold and weather) and lay me down behind a Rock, having by my reckoning travell'd nearer 40 miles than 30 in that day.

I awoke to find the day well on and Dundee departed. Which circumstances troubled me not one whit, there being only one Way thorough the Mountains and that in plain view, a deep Pass running straight North-west from the Loch's Head on the farther side. Breaking the Ice on the surface of a frozen pond, I scoop'd up water in the Pannikin to mix with Meal and so broke my fast, then made my way (passing sore and stiff) down to the Water. The mists of yesterday being all gone, I could see verie clear stretching away before me and to my left hand, a Row of Mountains like to a Monstrous Wall (and were indeed the North side of a great Valley), exeeding High and Steep; and rising above all, one Vast and Horrid Top, all seam'd with Fearfull Crags and Gulleys fill'd with Snow – the Pico or Master-Hill, as 'twere.

In about the space of two hours I am come to the Summit of the Pass, and descending on the other side it seems I am enter'd into a different, kindlier World. For there far below me is a Green Hollow where two Rivers meet, and descending further I see the Smoak of Houses, Greening Trees, Sheep with their little Lambs upon the hill, and hear the distant sound of Human Voices, and feel the soft Sea-Airs upon my cheek. And of a sudden I feel like to Moses which was suffer'd to see the Promis'd Land but not to enter therein; for I must continue to skulk and hide in Solitarinesse, like to a hunted Beast, within sight and sound of my Fellow-Creatures where is Warmth and Love and Shelter, which are deny'd to me. Belike the cause is Weaknesse and Fatigue from my Privations of the day before, but my Spirit seems to break within me and sinking down upon the ground I weep long and bitterlie.

Then I pray to God that he give me Strength to continue in my Task; and by and by, something recover'd, I am resolv'd to Play the Woman (I having always held that Women be as fitted as Men to perform all Things which Men presently hold to be proper to their Sex alone). I cast about me for a Shelter'd Spot wherefrom I may spy upon Dundee unobserv'd, the establishing of a Secure Base being as I believe the first Principle of War. With my Perspective I observe two things which in conjunction will supply that Want, Viz,

1. Dundee's Camp is presently a-pitching on that green level Place where the Rivers meet (which I see from Sandie's Map are Spean and Roy).

2. Here and there on the hillsides stand clusters of Huts, seeming-emptie for no smoak issues therefrom. These I take to be Sheilings, which I've heard do provide Shelter for the People in Summer when the Cattle are driven to the High Pastures.

I resolve, come Darknesse, to steal across to one of these Huts o'erlooking Dundee's Camp and there set up my Generall Head-Quarters as 'twere. In the mean time, there being nothing more I can accomplish to that end, I settle me down behind a Great Rock and write in my Journall all that hath transpired since my departing from Glen-Lyon.

—o-o-o—

Dundee's forced march from Angus to Glen Roy via Rannoch, was begun on the 14th of May and ended on the 16th! This must surely rank as one of the most heroic journeys in History – comparable to the achievements in the same field, of Xenophon, Hannibal, Caesar or Montrose. Anyone interested in the details, will find them recorded in the 'Grameid' – the heroic poem in Latin about his hero's adventures, written by young Philip of Amrycloss, Dundee's standard-bearer who accompanied him on the journey. (See Appendix: John Graham of Claverhouse.) For Aphra Behn, the rigours incurred by sharing the last stage of Dundee's journey, were to overtax her physical resources (already undermined through recurring bouts of her 'old sicknesse', and lead to a breakdown in her health.

10.

'I RESOLV'D I WOULD STEAL INTO DUNDEE'S CAMP'

Glen-Roy,
25th May, 1689.

ON THE DAY of my arriving in Glen-Spean, so soon as it was dark enough to venture safelie abroad, I made a great Cast along the hillside to the eastwards to avoid any outlying Piquets. This was accomplish'd with great Ease by reason there is here a fine Road, broad, firm and level! 'Tis mighty curious, and as to who made it or when, I can make no guess. Saving that, to my knowledge they were never in this Part of Scotland, one would have said 'twas the work of the old Romans. Belike 'tis call'd the Devil's Road or the Giants' Road* or some such, being so named in the Superstitious Middle Age; one thing's certain, 'twas never made by Highlanders.

Descending into the Valley I came to the banks of Spean. But O what a dreadfull Check was here, and for this cause: what, from high up on the hill-side had look'd to be but a Trifling Matter, was here plainlie seen to be an Insuperable Difficultie, for Spean was a Wild and Rushing Torrent, which to essay to wade across would be

* It was in fact then called 'The King's Hunting Road' being one of several so named – the famous 'Parallel Roads'. (see Notes).

to drown. (You should understand that being in what sea-men call High Latitudes, 'tis never, what we would say, Pit-Dark at this Season, and so I could discern what lay before me pretty Plain.) I walk'd along the bank searching for a spot where I might peradventure cross by stepping from Rock to Rock, and so came to a deep and exceeding narrow Gorge, where dark Crags fring'd with trees did so shut in the Flood that it here became a Raging Tumult, dashing 'gainst rocks in Fountains of Spray, and with a Horrid Booming that did set my knees a-tremble.

I was nigh to despairing when of a sudden I espied that which would furnish me with a Bridge, a tall uprooted Pine-tree which had fallen as to lie athwart the Gorge. A thrill of Horror went through me as I clamber'd upon the trunk; then, fixing my eyes on a Rock on the farther side, and shutting my mind against the Fearfull Peril of my Situation (to think on which would cause me such Distraction and Giddinesse as must make me either to lose my Footing or turn back), I began to walk across. Half-way, the tree did tremble and give a little Roll, that for a Terrible Moment I thought I was lost, but it checking its Motion, I did complete the Passage at a rush, and so stepp'd safe on the farther side.

Scrambling up the steep hill-side before me, I came by and by to another of those wonderfull Roads, which I follow'd to the westwards, it leading me to the hill-side in Glen-Roy overlooking Dundee's Camp. I cast about me until I found one of those Sheilings I spake of, the position whereof I'd earlier mark'd. Tho' the rudest Shelter imaginable being but a meer Booth of Turf and Stones, 'twould yet serve my Purpose exellentlie well. In I crawl'd and wrapping myself in my Plaid did fall immediately into a Profound Slumber.

The next day I awoke fever'd and with aching limbs. Filling the Pannikin with water from a little stream that ran close by, I moisten'd some Oat-meal, but on attempting to eat did retch violently and was seiz'd with such a Fit of Shudd'ring I felt I was like to die. By which I knew my Old Sicknesse to be upon me, brought on belike by the Rigours of my Journey. I would fain have lain down and slept (which, lacking Physick was to me the surest way to Recoverie) but Dutie constrain'd me to the carrying out of my Task; which however was nothing Onerous, meerly requiring that I keep a close Watch. From my Eyrie as 'twere, I had an Excellent Prospect of Dundee's Camp, being able to see through my Perspective Glasse verie plain: the Tents, the Horse-lines and the Sentries (even to the Facings of their Coats). No others were astir, belike taking their Rest after their Arduous Journey.

By and by, the day being worn on to afternoon, I hear a distant Noise of Bag-pipes which grows ever louder, then I espy men a-moving down Glen-Spean from the east. Looking at 'em through the Glasse, I see that these are Clans-men, in Blue Bonnets and Belted Plaids, each with a Round Buckler and girt Sword, some with Muskets or Halberts* besides; some there be a-horseback in glitt'ring Panoplie of gold-laced Coat, Breastplate and plumed Helmet, these I take to be their Chiefs. And all that day and in the days thereafter the Clans come down Glen-Spean and Glen-Roy (and I daresay from other Parts which I could not reach with my Glasse); making for some point to the west-wards which I could not see, but which I thought could not be afar off by reason their Camp must necessarilie be near to Dundee's. Severall times I espy a verie tall man with Moustachios, dress'd in the Trews and with an arm'd Retinue come a-riding into Dundee's Camp, and I wonder to myself if this can be that great man Sir Ewen Cameron which Colin Du spake of.

* Probably long-bladed Lochaber Axes.

And now my Sicknesse waxeth dailie apace, that at times I can scarce hold the Spy-glasse steadie such is my shaking. But yet I must be up and doing, for this Intelligence must somehow be convey'd to MacKay (who at the last reckoning was in Inverness), also what Dundee's Strategie is and the day of the Clans' Departing. And so I resolv'd that this verie night (it then being the 24th of May) I would steal into Dundee's Camp there to discover what I may, touching upon this last Foot.

The sun being gone down, I drop Sandie's Razor in my pocket (for want of other weapon) and descending the hill-side approach the Camp as softlie as I may. A little thin Rain is a-falling which doth aid me, none stirring abroad without they have good cause. You may be sure that before setting out, I've been diligent to mark where are their Piquets; wriggling on my Bellie like to a Serpent, and moving by Degrees verie slow and cautious, at last I am come to their Camp. Moving up to a Tent wherein is a light and from which issues the sound of Men's Voices, I listen with my ear to the Hem of the tent where is a space betwixt it and the Ground. They play at Cards, which Diversion lasts a wearisome time, but by and by these are put aside and they fall to talking of other Matters. Then my heart gives a bound for one asks, when does the Host begin a-marching on MacKay in Badenoch?

—Aiblins* he'll no be there, (says another). —Ye ken yon Colonel Ramsay, him that set oot frae Embro wi' the lave** o' the Scots Brigade, and whilk was tae meet wi' MacKay in Badenoch? Aweel, the News are just cam in — he was that feart o' meetin wi' ony wild Hielandmen on the Road, he's turned himsel' aroond and is e'en now linkin' awa back tae Perth. The fushionless Gowk!***

* Perhaps
** Rest
*** Gutless idiot (to give a colloquial translation).

—And what o' MacKay? (says the first).

—I dinnae ken whit he'll dae, Man, (says t'other). —Belike he'll be for joinin' wi' young Captain Forbes whilk is holdin' Ruthven Castle.

—May be ye're richt, (says a third). I jalouse* Johnnie-lad'll be ettlin'** tae be there afore MacKay, for tae bid him Welcome.

—So we're for Strath Spey then, in the morn, think ye? (says the second).

To which inquirie there was generall Agreement; also was there mention made of a great Muster on the morrow of the assembled Clans, at a spot call'd Dalcomera or Macomera where Spean meets with Lochy, being a Plain a few miles to the westwards. The talk now turning to Matters Soldierly, Viz, Wenching and Drinking, I thought it time to take my Leave.

As I creep back softlie from the Camp, I consider this Intelligence I've learn'd of, and perceive immediately 'tis of great Import for these Reasons:

1. Being disappointed of the Troops sent to aid him, MacKay is presently in Peril should Dundee come up with him. (I suppose the soldier to have signified Dundee when he spake of 'Johnnie-lad'.)

2. Dundee with the Highland Host is to march for Strath Spey on the morrow, or so 'twould appear.

3. MacKay and Dundee, both, do intend belike to reach Castle Ruthven; so the Race is to the swifter.

My plain Dutie then is to contrive to win to Ruthven Castle while it is yet in friendlie Hands, to advize Captain Forbes of Dundee's Design, that he may likewise warn MacKay. But O what Despair now fills me, for how I am

* Reckon
** Aspiring.

to accomplish such a Journey when I am so sick, I cannot think; yet attempt it I must.

I am now almost got clear of their Camp and am beginning to think myself safe when of a sudden my Hand knocks against something and there is a mighty Clash and Clatter (belike of Cooking-pots which I've overset) and a Voice at a little distance calls,

—Who goes?

I lie still hoping to escape being seen, but along comes the Sentrie, and espying me (for as I said 'twas not right dark) points his Carabine and calls again, —Who goes?

I spring up swiftlie and make to fly, whereat he aims his Piece; there is a little Click, by which I know his Carabine to have misfir'd (the Powder in the Pan belike being wetted by the Rain). Cursing, he drops his Firelock and reaches for his Sword, but as he tugs it from the Scabbard I pluck the Razor from my pocket, and flicking it open do sweep the Blade across his Throat. 'Twas as if a Black Mouth had of a sudden gaped open in his Gorge, then a Sheet of Blood spurts forth; he falls, his Feet kick the ground then he lies still. Tho' near to swounding with the Horror of what I've done, I compel myself to drag the bodie to the bank of Roy and there tumble it into the Water. I tell myself that if it be not found before the Clans depart on the Morrow, all may yet be well, perchance his Fellows believing him to have deserted, or gone to keep a Tryst with a Wench; which are but fond hopes, I think. My best Chance lieth in this: what with the Muster and Departing of the Clans on the Morrow every bodie will be so busy as to have no time to make diligent search for one Soldier gone a-missing.

And now there comes upon me such a Dreadfull Sense of Illnesse, also Confusion of Mind, that I know not rightly how I made shift to get back to my Hut. But reach it I did, and ent'ring therein fell straightway into a Swound.

When I awake 'tis broad Day; I am Clear in my Head and my Sicknesse something abated, but when I attempt to stand upon my feet, my legs do give from under me that I sprawl upon the Ground. But weak or no, I must essay to win to Ruthven Castle before Dundee and the Host arrive there. Looking at Sandie's Map I perceive Ruthven Castle to lie many miles to the east; to reach it I must follow Spean to its source at Loch Laggan whence, north a little way and to the eastwards, I will find the Head-waters of Spey which will lead me to Glen-Spey and so to Ruthven. The distance looks to be at least the equal of that Terrible Journey from the Mountain to Lochaber. In a kind of Extasy of Despair (knowing in my Heart my Strength will not suffice to carry me one Quarter of that Distance) I gather up my Gear 'gainst setting off, when of a sudden I hear a distant Whistling (verie faint), and the Blood rushes in my Veins for the Air is something familiar. I hearken again, the Whistling by Degrees waxing louder; 'tis *Lilliburlero*!

Sicknesse having caus'd my Mind to be distracted, for a moment I am assail'd by Deadlie Terror, conceiving the Whistler to be poor Sandie's Shade. But 'tis only for a moment; mastering myself, I go to the entrance of the Hut and give back *Newcastle*. Then my Heart gives a great Bound for Joy; for from behind a Heather-bush there rises a Head, and which smiles at me, a Head moreover I know well, ebony-skinn'd with tight-curled woollie Hair. 'Tis Samuel! As to our Discourse, and what arose therefrom, I must delay to write of that for a space, being Ill and Wearie. And so I end here for this present, it being the morning after Samuel's Happy Return.

11.
' INTELLIGENCE FROM BADENOCH '

Glen-Roy,
10th June, 1689.

I WRITE NOW in my Journall to make up the Tally of days until this time, being unable to perform the main part of this Task earlier, by reason I have perforce had to wait for News from Samuel, which News are set down under the third of these following Heads:

1. Samuel's Adventures

Fletcher, by reason of his Promise to myself (also from the Humanity of his Nature) did play his Personage upon the Magistrates of Edinburgh to such good purpose that, upon his coming to an Accomodation with the owner of the Cole Pit (by which I daresay Fletcher's purse was left the lighter), they caus'd Samuel to be releas'd. Fletcher meanwhile takes the boy into his own care, and perceiving him to be mightie diligent in all things he doth perform and moreover verie apt to learn (and has besides some understanding of the Irish tongue from his Sojourn in Argyll with his Scotch Master), Fletcher resolves to send Samuel to follow after me, being something troubl'd by not receiving further Intelligence by Sandie from myself. So off Samuel is sent (in Guise of Running Footman) to make Inquiry of me and to search me out; and is furnish'd with names of Persons in Fletcher's Employ (or Foe's? or the Doctor's? peradventure) which might furnish him with Intelligence sufficient to enable him to find me.

And so, as they might be Marks upon a Coast by which a Navigator shall shape his Course, Samuel did travel from my lodgings in Dundee to those in Dunkeld (both being kept by Persons on Fletcher's List; by the way, my Gear in Dunkeld is held safe), then to the Man into whose care Sandie had entrusted his Pack-horse Train, then to Colin Du in Glen-Lyon, and the Bowman's Wife, and after that through Rannach (where severall Folk in the Clachans had espied me), and so at last to Glen Spean (in which Place Colin Du had said perchance I might be found, tho' I had told him nothing of my Plans). Being arriv'd in Glen Spean, Samuel reasons to himself what Coign of Vantage I would choose whence to spy upon Dundee's Camp, and so had discovered my Sheiling. And that none too soon, for had I set out sooner on my Journey to Ruthven, we had not met; my Venture perforce would have fail'd utterlie and myself belike have died in the Mountains and my Bones ere now pick'd white by Eagles.

Perceiving me to be verie sick in Bodie and distracted in my Mind, Samuel prevail'd on me that I take to my Bed (such as it was, being a meer Mattress of Heather Boughs) wrap't in my Plaid, and after learning from me all that I purpos'd to accomplish, did himself go in my Room. (About which more hereafter.)

N.B. For his Gear in the Part of Spy, Samuel did take: Provision of Oat-meal, a small Pot, a Blankett, a Case-knife (all which things he had with him), also Sandie's Map which I have loan'd him.

2. The Highland Host

Samuel being departed on his Errand, and I vastlie comforted in my Mind (also overjoy'd to see my young Friend again and know he is freed from Servitude) did fall a-sleep, from which Slumber I was wak'd by the noise of Bag-pipes. And crawling to the entrance of my Hut did see the Highland Host advancing eastwards along Glen Spean. And looking through my Perspective observ'd the following, mightie plain: in the Van a bodie of Highlanders accompanied by some thirty Horse; then my Lord Dundee in Scarlett Coat and with Green Leaves in his Hat, a-riding with his Troop; then Companie upon Companie of Clansmen, for the most part huge and sturdy of limb, of Aspect Fierce and Awefull, brave in brightly chequer'd Plaids, with Targes on back and Broadswords on hip, and numb'ring by my reckoning close on four thousand men; the Chiefs a-horseback in Armour Antique but Splendid; Gay Banners streaming; the wild Music of their Pipes sending forth such a Martial Noise as would stir the blood of the dullest Clod-poll in Kent.

Never in my life did I think to see such a Sight, which I think must resemble those Barbarian Hosts that did break asunder then destroy the mightie Roman Empire. And my Heart fail's me, for I think that if they be properly manag'd, these men must surely be at the first invincible, being bred to War, and loving nothing so much as Fighting, and their whole Societie design'd as 'twere only for this End and Purpose. And should they gain a Victorie, and King James come over from Ireland, what then? Bloodie Civill War, even as the Doctor hath foreseen; but in the end William of Orange must surely prevail for he hath all the wealth of England and the Southern Parts of Scotland, and the Generall Support of the People to sustain him, and if his Armie be beaten, why, he can build it up anew; but let Dundee be beaten but the once and King James's

Cause is lost. Besides, the Nature of the Highlanders will not suffer 'em to stay overlong in the Field, for they must always be at their Businesse of Reiving and Plundering, and besides have the managing of their Crops and Cattle to attend to. However, this I will allow: 'tis not un-conceivable that with the aid of Dundee, King James might yet enjoy His Own again in Scotland; but that were to sunder the Kingdom, which must be to the Perpetuall Hurt of both Nations (and lead perchance to a Recurrence of those Dismall Bloodie Wars which for long harm'd both Scottish and English men), and a Thing infinitely to be regretted.

All these Reason'd Considerations notwithstanding, I own my Heart did go out to Dundee and I could almost wish that he succeed, for he and his Gallant Host do signify: Honour, Courage, Loyaltie, Nobilitie of Spirit and Sacrifice of Self to True Dutie, the maintaining of which Principles I've always held should constitute the Chiefest Care of a Man or a Woman.

3. Intelligence which Samuel hath brought me from Badenoch

i. May 28th. Dundee pitcheth Camp in Glen Spey, a little distance from Ruthven Castle which is held by Forbes for MacKay.

ii. May 29th. This being the Birth-day of King Charles II, Dundee caus'd lit a Bonfire with much celebration; which being over, Keppoch invests Castle Ruthven. Generall MacKay who is close by at Alvie, being expected to relieve the Castle, Capt. Forbes delays surrend'ring it; but MacKay not appearing, he is compell'd to surrender as he hath given his Word so to do if he be not relieved in three days.

iii. Ruthven being set afire, Dundee essays to come up with MacKay who (by reason Ramsay hath not joined Forces with him) flees down Glen-Spey.

iv. June 5th. Dundee resteth for a day at the Mouth of Glen-Spey, MacKay having escap'd him and won to the Low lands beyond the Glen, there being join'd by Berkeley's and Leslie's.

v. Dundee, perceiving he dare venture no further by reason that on that flat open Countrie the Clans could never stand 'gainst Horse, and MacKay's Strength now being much augmented, resolved to return to Lochaber, which he does, arriving on the 10th of June. (The Clans-men being cumber'd with Plunder which they wish to take back to their homes and will not be stay'd therefrom, Dundee is compell'd to disband the Host for a space. And to the end that MacKay not fall upon him in this Pass, hath cunningly contriv'd that MacKay discover False Intelligence, Viz, King James hath cross'd from Ireland and is presently a-landing Troops and Munition at Inverlochy in Lochaber. MacKay, believing this to be true, hath abandon'd the Pursuit and is for Inverness, whence 'tis rumour'd, he purposes to return to Edinburgh.)

P.S. Samuel hath won Golden Opinions from me for the Dilligence and Cunning he hath shown in the Part of Spy. Arriving at Ruthven betimes, he was able to advise Forbes early of Dundee's coming, Forbes then sending an Express to MacKay with that Intelligence. Severall times Samuel did steal into the Enemy Encampment where from Discourse overheard (much being in the Irish Tongue of which he hath some fortunate Understanding) he made shift to interpret something of their Plans. Which being communicated to MacKay, he was able to elude Dundee and at the last win clear. Only, MacKay's later Withdrawal (on the Generall learning of King James's supposed Landing) being so incontinent, Samuel was not able to advize him as to how Matters truly stood.

P.P.S. Samuel is verie diligent to minister to me in my Sicknesse, doing all things needfull and that with such Charitie and Chearfullness, as makes me like to weep for Gratitude, and I pray God to bless him. (All the time he was absent in Badenoch, I verie ill and shiv'ring; oft tormented beyond endurance by Clowds of stinging Midges; not stirring from the Hut save at night for purposes of Nature and to collect water in the pannikin; frighten'd almost to Death with the Apprehension of my Condition, to be sick and no Help; prayed to God but scarce knew what I said or why, my Thoughts being all confus'd.)

12.

' A DESP'RATE PASS '

Glen-Roy,
About the Middle of July, 1689.

THE ENEMY DRAWS NIGH and Time is short. Samuel is presently on the Hill a-keeping Watch. I've writ Letters to Fletcher and MacKay which Samuel will deliver and he can win to Colin Du. While I wait for Samuel to bring me Intelligence of them that seek me, I write in my Journall concerning what hath happen'd here since Samuel return'd from Badenoch. All Intelligence hath perforce been garner'd by Samuel, myself being not able to stir abroad by reason of my Sicknesse. Besides, a Boy being Active and Small may go where a grown Man or Woman could not, and Samuel's skin being black doth aid concealment; in a word he performs the Businesse better I daresay than I could myself, and I were able. (Also he hath, at no small risk, replenish'd our store of Meal from their Supply.)

Until of late I have been so sick and my Mind so confus'd as not to have been able to write anything at all. And by these same causes, my Memory of all this time being something imperfect and disorder'd (in witness whereof: I've so lost my reckoning of Time as no longer to be certain of the day of the month), I can write this

Account but in Generalls, the which I now set down in Severall Sections under one Head, Viz,

Intelligence which Samuel hath brought me in Lochaber
1. Dundee remaineth in Lochaber

The Highland Host being disbanded for the mean time, and MacKay belike return'd to Edinburgh, Dundee stays in Glen-Roy with his Troop.

2. Dundee traineth the MacLean's; he doth write many Letters

Sir Alexander MacLean with 400 of his Clan doth arrive in Lochaber from the Western Islands. These Clans-men being fresh, and not being distracted with Plunder, Dundee retains 'em and spends all day a-teaching 'em to stand 'gainst Horse, a thing most un-naturall to Highlanders. And by night he writeth Letters, and never seems to stay from Writing, for the Light in his Tent doth never cease to burn in the night and in the morning there are always Letters giv'n out to Bearers, as many as 10 or 20 at one time. Which correspondence I suppose to be address'd to the Chiefs, against the Clans' Assembling at some further time.

3. Dundee is accounted a Great and Famous Man by the Highlanders

In spite of him failing to catch and beat MacKay in Glen-Spey, Dundee's Name is now become famous throughout the Highlands, for with but 50 men and no money and no Commission, he hath rais'd an Armie and led Prince William's men a Merrie Dance. And his Repute and Standing are assur'd among the Highlanders, they mightilie admiring and loving him for his Cheerfull Endurance of all the Hardships of the Campaign (he sleeping no whit the softer nor eating daintier than any of his men) and for his Friendlinesse and Care towards 'em.

4. The Clans summoned to assemble on July 29th

Dundee's Commission at last arriving from Ireland, he can now command where before he must cajole, and 'tis bruited about the Camp-fires that the Clans are summon'd to assemble on the 29th of July, tho' where this is to be Samuel was not able to discover. (By the way, Dundee with many of his Troop do from time to time remove themselves from Glen-Roy, belike to ease the Dutie of their Host Lochiel in supplying 'em with Provision. And – perforce for this same cause is their Camp something diminish'd at this time of writing.)

5. Lord John Murray is come to Athole

Lord John Murray is but lately arrived in Athole (which Colin Du had advis'd me was toward) to dissuade the Clans-men there from rising for Dundee. Dundee 'tis said writes Letters (some of 'em Expresses) continually to Lord John at Pitlochry urging that he consider wherein his true Dutie lieth, which is to serve King James.

But now of a sudden, Fortune's Wheel hath turned against me. For this verie morning comes Samuel to the Hut betimes, with these Dismall Tidings:

–Sir, says he, –there are come into Glen Spean from the West three Men I like not the look of.

At this my Heart gives a Start and with Melancholie

Foreboding I ask if one be verie tall and thin, and wears a Cloke of Dark Colour.

—Aye, Sir, replys he, —that is him to the Life.

—And the others, (I inquire), —are they clad in Lowland Habit?

—E'en so, Sir, (returns Samuel). —Why, have you seen 'em afore then?

—Nay, Samuel, but I knew one that did, and died thereby.

And I told Samuel that we were in a Desp'rate Pass and that he must be the Bearer of Letters for Fletcher and MacKay which I should presently write, and which he must make shift to take to Colin Du, who would see to their Dispatching.

—But, Sir! cries Samuel in Dismay, I cannot leave you here!

—You can and you must; I say, speaking firm yet gentle, for the Lad begins to weep. And I reason with him that 'tis impossible I should accompanie him, being not sufficiently recover'd as to have any hope at all of out-running Pursuit; and besides, my staying must increase his hopes of winning clear, for belike they search for but one Person and that myself.

Then I tell him all of my Design that he may fully know what Great Matters hang upon his reaching Colin Du, and a-purpose touch on the Danger of his Journey and the Honour and Glorie to be gain'd therefrom. And by and by he quite cheers up, for a Lad of Spirit loves nothing so much as an Adventure whereby he can prove himself: whether Robbing an Orchard or Rescuing a Princess, it matters not overmuch.

All the above I've writ in my Journall while Samuel keeps watch, also writing Letters to Fletcher and MacKay, and urge the latter that he come North without delay in consideration of the Clans' Assembling on July the 29th. And now Samuel comes again to the Hut and says that the Men have been to Dundee's Camp, and are presently abroad again with many others, and they do begin to climb the Hill-side in long Ranks, like Beaters at a Hunt.

—Go now, Samuel; I say (beginning to be sore afraid but keeping a Cheerfull Countenance for the Lad's sake); and I give him Sandie's Satchel with the contents thereof. And in a moment more, I shall give him this my Journall for safe keeping, and I fear I shall never see it, or my dear young Friend again.

—o-o-o—

For the reader to visualize Aphra Behn's route in the next chapter, reference to a map might be useful — the Map in the text for Part Two: the river Roy to Blair via the river Spean, Laggan and the river Garry; or sheets 36, 37 and 48 in the old Ordnance Survey 'One Inch' series. (In the text Map 'Loch Eggan' is a mis-spelling for Loch Laggan and 'Strowan' is the modern Struan — the scene of her incarceration.) For details concerning the 'raison d'etre' of Dundee's absence from Glen Roy and his movements in Glen Garry, see the notes for Chapter 14.

13.
' MADAM WILL YOU TALK? '

Dunkeld,
26th July, 1689.

HAVING BY GOD'S MERCIE escap'd from mine Enemies and being safe arriv'd in Dunkeld (where I'm install'd in my old Lodgings), I do set down in my Journall what hath befell me after Samuel's departing for Glen-Lyon.

I awaited the Enemy with what Composure I could summon (it being un-conceivable they'd not find me and they employ the same Logic Samuel did to discover my Hiding-place), and by and by did hear many Voices on the Hill below, and soon after there burst into the Hut some Wild Highlanders which laying violent hands on me did drag me forth by Main Force (tho' there was no necessitie for that, as Resistance being vain, I'd have obey'd a Summons to remove myself).

Being abroad, I look'd around me for the Fatal Three and espied 'em standing a little way off from the other Beaters (these being chiefly Clans-men, also some of Dundee's Dragoons). Of the Three, two were fellows of the Common Sort, but the third was even as Sandie had describ'd, being so muffl'd in his Dark Cloke that no part of him could be descried, not even his Face, that being shrouded in a great Hood which shadow'd all his features. Verie straight and still stood he, appearing in my Fancie like to a verie Spectre of Death, as to cause a Deadly Fear to clutch at my Heart. (You will, and you are charitable, remember that I was but new-risen from a Sick-bed and my Mind yet apt to be possess'd by Maggots.) Never a word spake he, yet 'twas evident, I know not rightly how, 'twas he which commanded.

On being got down from the Hill-side (which I accomplished with much Pain and Difficultie by reason of my Limbs being long un-accustom'd to Exercise), I was set upon a little nag, just such a one as Colin Du had lent me, my feet tied beneath its belly and my hands bound in front of me so was able to grasp the Bridle. I had, I suppose (such is our Naturall Self-esteem), thought to be taken instanter to Dundee and was something surpriz'd when, leaving Dundee's Camp in Glen-Roy behind, the Three with myself did set off Eastwards up Glen-Spean, me riding betwixt the two Varlets, and their Master at some distance to the fore. (His Garb did cause me to conjecture: was he perchance some Papistickall Spy or Emissary from Douai, presently employ'd in the service of King James?)

I minded me that 'twas my Dutie to observe and note the twists and turns of our Road, that I might know whither we travell'd, but tho' I essay'd to do this at the first, I was so weak from my recent Sicknesse and from lying abed so long and besides being distracted by Discomfort from the jolting of the saddle, that I fell at last into a kind of Stupor or Waking Swound, as to be sensible only in Generall of my Surroundings. (Touching which, all I can rightly recall is that after skirting a Dark and Lonely Loch, our Road for the first part trended through a broken Desert Countrie, subsequently running in Valleys enclos'd by Gloomie Hills, at one point going thorough a long Pass where the Mountains arose Steep and Frightfull on either hand.) Our direction so far as I could tell from the sun (which for the most part was hid from view, the Weather being Dank and Mistie all the while) trended to the East and something to the South. How far we travell'd I could in no wise say with any Exactnesse, but as we journey'd without Stay until the setting of the sun and for some considerable time thereafter, I should guess the Distance to have been something betwixt forty and sixty Miles. As to the Cause of the Journey, and why we should be removing ourselves so far from Dundee's Camp, I could make no Guess.

At length, the sun being long gone down, we halted at a straggling Clachan. Here we dismounted, my bonds were untied and I was led (carry'd would be nearer truth for I was so stiff and fatigu'd as scarce to be able to stand) to a long building appearing something more substantial than the rest, and cast therein. Here, by the light of a lant-horn was I stripp'd and my Sex discover'd, whereafter I was suffer'd to dress again, my captors then departing. The last thing I heard before falling into a Slumber of Compleat Exhaustion was the Squeaking of a Key being turn'd in the Lock.

I wak'd to find myself in a stone building which I reckon'd had at one time been a Byre or Stable, for along one wall were Stalls and above 'em windows (verie small) thorough which a pale sunlight issu'd. The building was now used as a Place of Storage, the wall opposite the stalls being lin'd with sacks (of flour or meal perchance?), also Casks and Boxes. The strength and Securitie of the building also the Abundance of Provision inclin'd me to think its Purpose might be Militarie. Something refresh'd by my sleep (tho' mightie chill'd and hungry for I had been giv'n neither Blanketts nor Food) I got upon my feet and forc'd myself to walk about, both to ease the Stiffnesse from my limbs and by exercising 'em to regain a little of their lost strength. Also, you may be sure, I examin'd the place exceeding close for any Means of escaping, but as you may guess found none. I then fell to searching for aught that could serve as a Weapon, and as I was employ'd in this exercise the Door was unlock'd and in came my three Captors, which for sake of Clarity in discoursing of, I shall designate thus: 1st Guard, 2nd Guard, Officer.

Without a word being said the 1st Guard takes me roughlie by the arms and I am forc'd to sit on a chair which the 2nd Guard carries and to which I am bound by my middle. A box is then dragg'd forth from the wall and set before me. Then their Officer (whose face I cannot see for 'tis hidden inside that Monstrous Hood), speaking in a Terrible Soft Whisp'ring Voice says to me in Ironie (from the Words of the Song),

—Madam will you talk?

I can feel my Heart a-beating in my Bosom and my Mouth is of a sudden parch'd such is my Fear, for I know well that and I remain silent, they'll not be gentle with me. But then I think on Carstares which endur'd the Thumbscrews, and Fletcher who sacrific'd all his Worldly Goods and Estate, and Sandie that died, all for the same Cause in which I now serve and I resolve I shall not fail 'em.

—You think to outface me? continued the Officer in that Serpent's Hiss. —Know you who I am? Belike you've heard of Major Snell, one of Kirke's Lambs at Tangiers?

At which disclosure my Fear doth wax the greater and that were possible. For as all the world knows, the name of Colonel Kirke became a by-word for Crueltie and Mercilessnesse at Tangiers, and the men of his Terrible Regiment, Queen Catherine's Own, were nam'd Lambs in

Ironie for the Paschal Lamb on their Appointments.* And of that Dreadfull Companie was none more steep'd in Blood and Wickedness than Major Snell, who 'tis said did roast his Prisoners alive on Spits (and whom indeed I'd revil'd in my Play, The Widow Ranter). And into this Monster's clutches was I now fall'n!

Then I minded me that Snell was reported kill'd at Sedgemoor Fight, and on my making this Objection, he rejoins,

—'Tis what the world believes. And 'tis in a Manner true, for to the world I exist no longer. At Sedgemoor, as Dr. Mews was shifting the Cannon to the Centre, a chance shot caused blow up a Powder Cask in the Train as it pass'd by me. Tho' horribly burnt and left for dead, I recover'd, an old peasant finding me after the Battle and his wife nursing me back to health in their cottage. Being recover'd, them I slew that none might discover I had not died. I then came to London, cloked as you see me now, and play'd my personage upon Lord Melfort that he made me his Chief of Intelligence, for these three Causes: Major Snell was believ'd dead and none could know that I was he, by reason of my Face being so hideously disfigur'd as not to be recognizable; and a man with no Past hath Infinit Advantage in the Trade of Intelligencing. Then, my Experience of Campaigning in Foreign Parts had furnish'd me with Skills proper to my Calling. Also, and perchance this was the Chiefest Cause of all, because of the Injuries I'd taken at Sedgemoor Fight, I hated the King's Enemies with a Steadie and Consuming Fire that can ne'er be quench'd. As you might, Madam, had you suffer'd thus.

And throwing back the Hood and thrusting forth his Hands, he stoop'd over me. I shriek'd in Horror for the Creature had no Face! Just a sear'd and pucker'd Plate of

* Insignia

Flesh, with a shrivell'd Slit for Mouth, and a pair of Gaping Holes where the Nose had been. One Eye was gone and its room a Pit; the other stared at me betwixt wither'd lids with a Steadie and Terrible Malevolence. The Hands were Meer Claws, like to the Tallons of a Bird of Prey, and did put me in mind of an Egyptian Mummy's Hands I'd once seen at Surgeons-Hall. And had he not been utterlie Evill, I could have felt Compassion.

Now did I truly know Despair, for Mercie and Pity were Strangers to this Man.

—Well Madam? Says he, thinking peradventure his Discoverie of himself to me hath frighten'd me into my Wits as 'twere. On my remaining silent he whispers, —and you will; and makes a Sign to the Guards.

The 1st Guard takes from his pocket a curious Engine which consisteth of two flat Bars of Iron in a Frame, they being join'd through their middles by a thick Screw. Then am I seiz'd with a Great Terror and my limbs begin to tremble, for tho' I've not seen this Instrument afore, yet I know 'tis the Thumbscrews.

The Machine being plac'd upon the Box before me, my Thumbs are put between the Bars and while the 2nd Guard holds my arms fast, t'other twirls the Knop of the Screw till my Thumbs be gripp'd firm. Then he continues to turn the Screw, but verie slow now. At first there's only a Sharp Throbbing or Pricking, but as by Degrees he tightens the Screw, this changes to a Hot Stabbing Pain, then to an Un-endurable Agonie. I had Ne'er imagin'd such a Pain could be; I hear myself screaming, then I must perforce have swounded away, for I find myself opening my eyes and am sensible that the Pain is less. The Guard perforce hath loosen'd the Screw; but now he tightens it again (and 'tis marvellous how little he needs to turn it) and the Agonie is as Terrible as before. Again I swound and on recov'ring, the Torture is again applied, and this happens altogether Three Times.

—Well, Madam, says Snell, when my Tormentors have done and my Bonds been untied and the Engine remov'd. —That was but the Prologue to the Play. Tomorrow we'll attend the First Act. 'Twill be passing strange methinks, if the Boot doth not help you find your Tongue.

—I can tell you Nothing, (I cry), —and I know Nothing.

—Madam, (says he — and his next words do confirm what all along I'd fear'd would come to pass), —do not try my Patience. The Bishop's* wagging tongue did furnish me with Scent as for a Hound. Long have I follow'd on your Track and would have found you ere now but for two Causes: the Rustick Clowns and Rude Mechanickalls assign'd to help me by Lord Melfort are but Sorry Tools in my hand; Melfort, I fear, is a Bungling Fool, yet I must use him for my Purpose, for he hath King James's ear. Also I've been abroad in Ireland these two months, my Skills being requir'd to seek out Intelligence of the Intentions of the Rebells in London-Derry. But now, Pretty Bird, you're in my Cage at last, and tomorrow you shall sing. And so, Madam, I bid you Good-day.

With which False Courtesie he departs with his Varlets.

For some time I am so distracted with the Pain in my thumbs and the Horror of imagining worse Tortures to come, that I think I became in a Manner Mad, for a Space. By and by however, coming to myself, and finding my Thumbs not to be so crush'd and mangl'd as I'd feared (and finding a Gloomie Satisfaction in being a Fellow-Martyr as 'twere with Carstares), I resolve on Three Courses:

1. to say Nothing, however Keen the Torment (having, you could say serv'd an Honourable Apprenticeship).
2. to continue to seek for Means of Escape, and

* Dr. Burnet was consectrated Bishop of Salisbury on March 31st 1689.

3. to make shift to furnish myself with a Weapon.
In the furtherance of which Tasks was I engag'd when I did hear a Noise of Horses' Feet and Voices and the Clatter of Accoutrements, and all outside my Prison is Bustle and Stir. And by and by my Prison Door is unlock'd and a Trooper enters accompany'd by the 1st Guard, who being asked sharply by the Soldier, was I the Woman? Replys sullenly, —'Tis so. Whereat the Trooper asks me (verie civill) to accompany him and it please me. And leads me forth into a pleasant Water-meadow (such as in Scotland is call'd a Haugh) beside a stream with Hills on either side, but not so Steep and Gloomie as those I recall'd from the day before. On the meadow were Tents a-pitching and Cooking-fires a-readying, and at some distance Horses being led across a Ford to their Lines beyond the farther Bank, so that what with the sun shining bright and clear 'twas as Cheerfull a Sight as you could wish to see, (which did but make my own Pass seem more Dismall by Compare).

My escort show'd me into a Tent in which an Officer in a travel-stain'd Coat was seated writing, a Drum set end-wise serving as Table.

—This is the Woman, Your Grace; announc'd the Trooper and withdrew.

The writer look'd up and I saw with a Start 'twas Dundee! How to describe the wonderfull Manlie Beauty of that Face, now something worn with Cares and Fatigue, border'd with Rippling Locks now streak'd with Grey, which I warrant had not been there when I'd seen him ride through Edinburgh. Dundee rises and waves me to a chair which hath been set ready. Making inquiry and I'd eaten or drunk, he sends the Trooper (who waits outside the Tent) for refreshment, and when I'd partaken, says, in a Voice Pleasant and Courtlie,

—I'm sorry and sham'd, Madam, you've been used so

ill; 'Twas done without my Knowledge or it had ne'er happen'd. Snell is Melfort's Creature so I cannot touch him, more's the pity, Melfort being next to the King. And Snell were answerable to me, he'd have hanged for this day's Work. But be assur'd Madam, there will be no more Torture; I've made it passing plain to Snell that, Melfort or no, his Life is forfeit and he commit such Barbaritie a second time.

And Dundee bends upon me a Look of Concern and Compassion, in which there's yet mingl'd something of Puzzl'd Reproach.

—Madam, continues he, in a Voice which tho' still Polite is become Stern, —I will be blunt with you. You are a Spy and the Usages of War demand that you be shot. You do not deny either the Charge or Knowledge of the Penalty?

On my assenting (for it were Profit-less to pretend other), he goes on: —I admire your Courage Madam and your Perseverance, but I own I am at a Loss to know why you undertook to spy against King James. And he gives me a Sorrowing Look, as a Lover might who asks of his Mistress why she has deceiv'd him. Which tells me I think that he knows who I am (yet forebears to say so), Aphra Behn's Love for her King being a Matter of Publick Knowledge.

—Sir, I reply, —I think perchance we are alike in this: we both serve our Master sincerely. But we differ in perceiving where His Good most lieth.

Dundee gives me a Searching Look (as to test the Honestie of my Opinion) and when he makes reply his Voice is kindlie;

—As to that, I can make no Judgement, except to say that a Belief sincerely held upon Grounds well-consider'd, is a Thing I can respect. In our Father's time, Cavalier fought Roundhead for just such Cause, and who is to say which had the less Honour thereby? Such Considerations notwithstanding, Madam, I must tell you I'm constrain'd to do my Dutie, even tho' 'twere painfull to me.

—You mean, (I reply in a trembling Voice as I perceive the Import of his words, for 'tis one thing to know your Life is in the Balances, another to be told 'tis to end), —I am to die?

Dundee paces the Tent, as he might be something troubl'd in his Mind, then he turns and faces me, his Brows knit.

—Madam, he says, his Voice sounding as if he strives to master some Strong Emotion, —in administ'ring the Law it hath always been my Care to temper the Application of Justice with Mercie, and Respect for the Law be not harm'd thereby. This much I will grant; in ten days I will pass this Way again and if then you will tell me all you have discover'd in your Spying, and give me your Word you'll take no further Part in that Businesse, you may go free. If not — He breaks off and smiles at me Grave and Sorrowfull, then concludes: —We understand each other Madam, I think.

I return his Smile tho' something tremulous, and I ask myself if I have ever met a Man so Honourable, so Compassionate, so Gentleman-like, and withall so Comelie as this? God help me, I could love this Man. And I begin to think that the Reports concerning Bloodie Claverhouse which revell'd in the Slaughter of Poor Innocent Covenanting Folk, are but Meer Inventions put about by his Enemies.

Dundee calls, the Trooper re-appears and returns me to my Prison (where I perceive are now Blanketts and a Pail to serve as Privy), and summons an Orderlie to salve and bind up my poor Thumbs.

And betimes on the morrow something to my surprize I am again summon'd to Dundee, whom I find at breakfast outside his Tent, in Buff-Coat and Boots, Sword girt and white-plumed Beaver-hat atop his fresh-curl'd Locks. After inquiring verie courteous and kindlie how I did and inviting me to break my fast with him, says he;

—My Businesse here detains me longer than I did expect — pray accompany me Madam while I inspect the Dispositions of the Camp. And sets off on foot alone save for myself.

We fetch a great Compass around the Camp (wherein are lodg'd but Dundee's own Troop of Lowland Horse and no Highlandmen) on high ground o'erlooking it, where Dundee hath Vedettes posted; and find all things excellentlie order'd, the Outposts readie and alert, the Watchword ('tis Forfar) demanded and given back right smartly. 'Tis verie evident to myself that the Soldiers did generally love their Commander, and I doubt not 'tis to their Affection and Confidence he owes that marvellous control he hath exercized over 'em under the most critical of Circumstances.

And as we walk, Dundee presses me (for mine own sake I think as much as for his Cause's Benefit) that I divulge to him the Intelligence I've earn'd of in my Spying. But, tho' sore tempted (for only a Fool yields up his Life without there be some verie pressing Cause) I hold my Peace.

—Verie well, Madam, (says he at length, seeing I am not to be drawn in this Matter), —you have yet nine days in which to change your mind, which I most earnestlie hope you will find Cause to do.

And falls to talking of other Matters and in a Manner so easy and so charming that any bodie o'erhearing must suppose us rather to be old Friends a-taking of the Air than Captive Spy and Enemie Commander burdened with a Thousand Cares. We talk'd of London and the Plays a-showing there last year, which he declar'd were for the most part poor stuff compar'd to my *The Roundheads* which he say'd he'd watch'd in the '82* when he'd sojourn'd in Town. Nor was this meer Idle Flatterie for he display'd a marvellous understanding of that Play (passing singular in a Plain Unvarnish'd Soldier which he is generallie conceiv'd to be) whose purpose was the Exposure of Hypocrisie.

—But I fear, Madam, Dundee continu'd, —that the Duke of Grafton paid but scant heed to your Exhortation; for I was with the King at Salisbury this November last when the News came in that Grafton and Churchill both, had gone over to the Prince of Orange.

(Which was mighty a subtil Observation, for my Dedication of the Play was to that same Duke of Grafton, and was in the form of a veil'd Warning as much to Monmouth as himself, 'gainst the temptation to usurp a Monarch's Throne, or to render Aid to them that might attempt such.)

Thus we continu'd, discoursing easily of a Thousand Things, my Lord Dundee showing such Wit, and Grace, and Knowledge cloked by Modestie (as is proper to a Gentleman that hath also some Learning and Refinement) that I own I was entirely captivated, as much by his Gallantry and Charm as by the Beauty of his Person. At last, being a little fatigu'd, we sat down to rest awhile by the steep banks of a Rill (what in Scotland is call'd a Burn) that came plashing down a Gulley in the hillside above us. On a sudden I hear a Bleating and looking up behold a Piteous Sight — a Ewe caught fast by her neck in the branches of a Birch-tree. The poor Beast's Plight was the more desperate for this Cause: she'd scant hold for her Feet saving a little narrow Ledge in the Sheer Face of Rock

* In Scotland at this time years were so designated, e.g. 'the '15', 'the '45'

that here form'd the Gulley Wall, so durst not struggle overmuch lest she slip and so fall, which should it come to pass must cause her to be strangl'd. 'Tis plain what hath occurr'd: in feeding too near the Gulley's Edge the Ewe had slipp'd and gone over (such mis-haps being verie common among Sheep from the Sillinesse of their Nature — as I should know that was bred in Kent).

—Can we not save the poor Creature? I implore Dundee. He shakes his head in Vexation and Amusement mingl'd.

—Madam, he replys, —were I to essay to put to rights every petty mis-chance that comes my way in the hurly-burly of a Martial Life, I warrant I'd have scant Leisure for the proper conduct of my Dutie. But be assur'd; the Shepherd will come a-seeking of his Charge by and by.

—Then Sir, (I return), —must he come incontinent, else he'll find his Charge be blinded; and I point to two Ravens that perch near to the Ewe. —Will the Intrepid Cavalier, (I continue), that scal'd the Crags of Edinburgh Castle refuse such a little Challenge? (And, tho' I strive to stay 'em, the Tears come a-welling in my eyes).

—Hold, enough! Madam, exclaims Dundee laughing, and casts his hands up in the Air in token of Surrender. —I yield! I yield! I have the Proof of Lead or so they say, but not of Tears I think.

And doffing his Sword-belt and Buff Coat, begins swiftlie to ascend the Sheer Face of the Rock (by cracks and ledges so small as to be scarce visible to myself) with as much Ease and Securitie, or so it seem'd, as he were climbing a Ladder. I mark the calm Fixitie of Purpose on his Face, and think he must have look'd so as a Boy when climbing of a Tree perchance, or tickling a Trout beneath a River-bank. Arriving at the place where the Ewe is entrapp'd, he pulls apart the boughs holding her neck;

whereat she scrambles up the Slope above her (which is less steep than that below) and so wins clear of the Gulley.

—Bravely done, Sir! I exclaim as Dundee returns to where I wait; —I thank you from my Heart.

And as I behold him, all flush'd and dustie from his Travail and laughing like to a carefree Lad with Prize of Plunder'd Apples, my Admiration and Gratitude bid fair to be displac'd by an altogether stronger Emotion. Tho' I seek to quench the Flame that Cupid with his fiery darts essays to kindle in my Breast (knowing there's no hope of Requitement for we're pledged to Causes that are Opposite, and his Lady Jean hath all Dundee's Heart, 'tis said), 'tis in vain; the Arrows, shot with all the Malice of an angrie God strike home and deep and I know myself fall'n victim to Love's sweet familiar Torment.

A heavie Dullness now comes upon me, quite driving out all my former Lightness and Gaiety of Spirit. Sensing which, Dundee seeks to engage me in Discourse no longer and we return in Silence to the Camp. Before summoning a Trooper to conduct me to my Prison he takes my hand in his, and in a voice of Tender Compassion says:

—Think well on my words to you of yesterday, Madam. Tho' I might wish it other, those must be my Terms. With all my Heart I do urge you that you examine verie close those Causes which you believe compel you to your present Dutie, and consider if perchance they be not mistaken. And now Madam, for the nonce — Farewell.

—o-o-o—

To My Lord Dundee, on the Occasion of Our Parting*

Like to a Planet circling round the Sunne,
Or a Reflected Image in a Glasse,
(Tho' they be Two, they are conjoin'd as One,
Yet never can their Union come to pass);
So by Desire to you I'm held in Thrall,
*But Dutie keeps our Courses Severall.***

The Moth that round the Candle's Flame doth flye,
The Coney that the Weasell's Gaze holds fast,
The Sailor captur'd by the Siren's Lay,
The Fish that riseth to the Lure at Last;
His Life, for Love, the Courting Spider pays –
Not less than these, my Heart ensnarèd is.

And now the Days, which are belike to be my last on Earth, begin to pass with a Terrifying Swiftnesse. And this is the Order they follow: I am brought Meat and Drink twice daily by one or the other of my Guards; I essay to find Means to make a Weapon, but in Vain; I walk up and down and exercise my Limbs to the end they regain something of their strength; my Thumbs heal by Degrees; I search the Room continuallie for a Way of Egress, but can discover none (be sure I've alreadie examin'd the Windows which are overlie Narrow to permit the Passage of a Man or Woman, also the Door which is Stout and Massive and is besides secur'd by a verie Strong Lock).

I resolve that whate'er happen, I'll keep silent. (For to do other were to put in Jeopardie the lives of Colin Du, of the Bowman and his Goodwife, of the Lodging-keepers

* I discovered this poem interleaved between two draft letters to Andrew Fletcher. Assuming it to have been misplaced, I inserted it here, as it seemed the appropriate place. (Transcriber)

** Separate

in Dunkeld and Dundee, of Samuel perchance, and, should Dundee prevail, of Fletcher and peradventure even the Doctor; and besides MacKay's Strategie would be put at Naught.) And if I die, why 'tis no Great Matter. I've no Chick nor Child nor Lover to mourn my Passing; my Muse is fall'n Silent, my Friends all Dead – Otway, Mightie Rochester, Buckingham, and Prettie Nell,* all I think do call me from their Graves to join 'em.

Mean-while, I exercise my Wits and Eyes 'gainst the Chance Discoverie of aught which I may turn to my Advantage. (By the Way, on my third Day in this Place, Dundee and his Troop depart as I could tell by the Stir and Noise of their Removing.) Whenever my Guards (which are arm'd with Pistols) do bring me Meat and Drink I essay to engage 'em in Discourse, thinking peradventure to earn something to my Profitt. One is mighty Sullen and will make no reply to my Remarks and Inquiries; this is he which I call the 1st Guard. But the 2nd Guard beginneth by Degrees to unbend and even in time to wax Loquacious, this being a Puffed-up Sillie Fellow methinks which fancies himself a Roaring Boy and loves nothing better than to Boast of his Mightie Exploits and he can find a Willing Audience (than which none more Willing than myself, you may be sure).

'Twas on the 5th Day of my Captivitie that the first Conception of a Plan came into my Mind, and it happen'd thus: During our Discourse (or rather his Soliloquy) it was the 2nd Guard's habit sometimes to take a Pipe of Tobacco. After severall Occasions I began idly to notice that he always took his Pipe to the Door. Chancing to think on this, it came to me of a sudden that perchance he did this for a Speciall Cause, which did lead me to

* Presumably Nell Gwyn, whom Aphra Behn greatly liked and admired and who died of apoplexy in 1688, aged thirty-eight.

inquire of myself, why should he not smoke his Pipe elsewhere in the Room than by the Door? And then the likelie Cause flash'd upon my Mind; and on examining the Stores rang'd along the Wall opposite the Door I soon found that which I suspected must be there, and ought to have thought on long ere now. (Perchance Snell's mention of the Cause of his Injurie had first lodg'd the Thought in my Mind, like to a Seed planted in the Earth.)

An Enterprize, like Love, doth feed on Hope, and now that I could see my Purpose plain, Viz, to bring together those Things which my Guard had taken Pains to keep apart (namelie Fire and Gunpowder), I made shift to devize a Plan, consisting of these Severall Sections:

1. My first Care in this must be the Blowing-up of the Powder Kegs in such a Manner as to breach the Building, yet not kill or injure myself.
2. To this End, I must find a Means to pierce one Keg, that I may lay a Powder-train to where it can be fired.
3. I must needs be diligent to conceal all Traces of my Labours.
4. I must, as for a Play, rehearse the Proper Motions I'll be making when I carry out my Plan.

Well, no doubt 'twas a Desp'rate Wild Scheme and like to miscarry at a Score of Points, but there being no Profitt in that kind of Speculation, I shut my Mind 'gainst the chance of Failure, and made shift to begin my Preparations. Searching among the Stores I found there to be in Toto, 5 Powder Kegs, each as would contain no more than a small Bucket. As to the Explosive Force to be occasion'd by their Blowing-up, of that I could make no Reckoning, but I guessed perchance three Kegs would suffice. The Kegs standing all together at the middle part of the Wall, I removed two to the furthest Corner opposite the Door and in their Room put Sacks of Grain.

After a little searching I found, driven into the Mortar of the Wall, an old rusty Nail (belike for the hanging-up of Harness formerlie) which by working back and forth I contriv'd to loosen and at last withdraw (which labour I accomplish'd but slowly by reason of my injur'd Thumbs). I then rubbed this Nail against the Wall that the point be made sharp and thus fashion'd me an Auger. Then I set to work to bore a Hole in one of the Kegs, which Task prov'd exeeding Difficult and Tedious by reason of the Tendernesse of my Thumbs, and the Hardnesse of the Wood and my Instrument having no Handle. However, by Degrees a Scratch became a Hollow and a Hollow a Hole, which did please me mightily causing me nigh as much Satisfaction (so it seem'd) as I had writ a Play. (And all this time I must needs dissimulate to my Guardians, which strange to say I found the easiest thing in the world, and indeed play'd my Personage on the 2nd Guard to such effect that he calls me his Marrow* and suffers me to share a Pipe with him; upon this last Accomodation doth a Main Part of my Plan depend.)

At last, after four Days' Labour, I felt the Wood beneath the Auger yield upon a sudden, then the Naile slips into the Keg and on my withdrawing it a trickle of Black Grains follows. Now my Heart begins to beat the faster (as I suppose MacBeth's to have done when he was persuaded to Duncan's Murther) for what hath until this present been only in the Mind, must now become translated into Act. So, screwing my Courage to the Sticking-place I lift the Keg and keeping next the Wall suffer a stream of Grains to run out behind me as I carry it to the Door. Replacing the Keg, I scatter Dust atop the Powder-train that it be not visible. Now is there naught to do but wait

* Boon companion; 'Mate' or 'Cobber' would be a colloquial equivalent.

(it being presently late in the afternoon); the time passes heavily, my Palms becoming Slick with Sweat and my Heart beating fast and light like to a Bird flutt'ring its wings within a cage. At last the Key turns in the Lock and in comes the 2nd Guard, bearing my Supper as is his wont.

As I eat, I make a Pretence of talking lightlie, but now the Time is come, the words stick something in my Throat, tho' the Guard seems not to notice my Distraction, prating on as to how, when a Sea-man in the Dutch Wars, he saved the Duke of York's life aboard the Royal Charles by his way of it. By and by he gets out his Smokeing Furniture and fills his Pipe (mightie slow and leisurely it seems). He strikes a Light, takes a Whiff or two then makes to pass the Pipe to me. Taking the Pipe in my Mouth I draw upon it hard to make sure the Coal burns bright, then stooping swiftlie, knock the Bowl out on the end of the Powder-train.

The Guard stares astonished as the Burning Tobacco drops upon the Ground; there is a Hissing as of an Angrie Serpent, then upon a sudden an exeeding bright Point of Light appears and races splutt'ring along the Wall. As I fling myself into a Stall, there comes a Blinding Flash, a Gust of Searing Air, and a Terrible Roar. I lie half-stunned while the Ground heaves beneath me and Things fly Whirring and Crashing all around. Then, saving a crackle of flames, there's Silence. I get upon my Feet and find myself to be unhurt; opposite me the Wall is quite beaten down, and above half the Roof is blown away. The Guard lies still upon the Floor, whether stunn'd or dead I cannot say; I take his Pistol and in a Trice am departed out of the Building.

The Clachan's in an Uproar, People a-running from their Houses in a mighty Taking, everywhere Smoak and Confusion, some Buildings next my Prison having taken Fire (from Blazing Beams falling on 'em, I suppose). 'Tis no Great Matter for me to slip away un-noticed; I come by and by to the Head-Dyke* which I clamber over, and thus hid follow it around to where it approacheth the River near to the Ford which I'd earlier observ'd. Thus far, my Thoughts being intirelie taken up with 'scaping, I'd not thought further as to what I'd do, and my Attempt succeed. My next Step was pretty plain however, and that was to put the Stream betwixt mine Enemies and myself and follow it down-stream, that is away from the Clachan. Also (and my Estimation of the Journey hither was aright) such a Course would take me towards the South-east, that is away from the Countrie of the Jacobite Clans towards those which were of Neither Partie. I wade across the Ford, then setting my face to the East (whereby the Sun is put behind me thus assuring me of my direction) I splash thorough a little Tributarie and set off down-stream.

There is here a Path so I make pretty good speed, and have travell'd above a Mile when I hear the sound of a Horse's Feet approaching from behind me. Turning, I see a Rider some way off but gaining fast. Now can I see him plain; 'tis Snell as I fear'd. For a moment Fear and Despair do fill me, then of a sudden these are quite driv'n out by a Sullen Furie at memorie of this Man's Wickednesse, and I resolve one or other of us must die. And with Resolve comes Coolness; drawing forth my Pistol, I see to the Priming then cock it. Tho' hating to harm a poor innocent creature, I aim at the Horse as being the surer Mark. Up Snell gallops, then observing I am arm'd essays to swerve; 'tis too late, I fire, the Horse checks as it had run against a Wall, then pitches head-long on the Road, flinging Snell from the saddle. As he scrambles to his knees, I rush upon him and with my clubb'd Pistol do smite him upon the

* An earthen wall separating the cultivated land round a settlement from the pastoral.

Head with all my Force. Again and again I strike and hear bone crunch yet keep on striking and a-striking until at last I am compell'd to cease from verie Exhaustion. He's dead without a Doubt for I observe his Skull to be all crush'd like to a stove-in Cask; and the Horse is dead too, poor Brute.

And as I press on, a great Numbness and Emptinesse of Spirit comes upon me. Which is why perchance, I fell all unsuspecting into an Ambuscade, two fellows in Highland Garb upon a sudden stepping from a little coppice of hazle-trees to stand in my Way. They chatter'd at me in their own Tongue and on my signifying that I had no Irish, signall'd for me to accompany them. Knowing 'twould be Profit-less to resist, I suffer them to lead me on, now sunk in a Dull Apathy as no longer caring greatlie if I had fall'n into the Enemie's Hands or no. In a verie little space, on turning a bend in the Way there opens before us an Arresting Prospect: a fair Park studded with Trees all glowing in the evening sun, and in the midst thereof a Mightie Keep, Tall and Massive and of such seeming strength as to be nigh impossible to take. In the Park a Great Encampment with Highlanders a-walking to and fro, and (which doth consummate my Miserie) streaming from the Castle Ramparts, the Royal Standard of King James!

I am conducted through the Camp to a Tent outside which a young Man dress'd in the Trews and gold-lac'd Doublet proper to a Highland Nobleman, talks with Clans-men. He shoots me an inquiring Gaze from keen Eyes set in a Face, square, resolute, and Manlie, tho' its Owner must yet be in his teens*.

* He was in fact barely fifteen years old; yet the following morning he led a successful revolt for the Atholl clansmen against Lord John Murray, they declaring for Dundee. Nearly sixty years later, he was executed for his part in the 1745 Jacobite Rebellion.

On my being brought before this young Man, he asks me my name, I giving back (as resolving to go down with all my Colours a-flying as 'twere),

—'Tis Thomas Johnson of London, Gentleman. (Which last must surelie have occasion'd some secret Mirth, for my Clothes are by this time become so worn and filthie, a Beggar would have scorn'd 'em.)

—Well, Mr. Thomas Johnson, reply's he, verie grave and civill, —and I am Simon Fraser of Lovat, at your Service. I trust these wild cateran* Sentries of mine show'd you no un-Politenesse. And you will be so kind as to accompany me, I shall e'en take you to my Chief.

And bowing, he conducts me to another Part of the Encampment, where he shows me into a fine Pavillion. Here an exceeding angrie Man in Chief's Attire argues with some others whose Rank I guess to be that of Gentlemen or Tacksmen such as Colin Du. Gloomilie I wait (belike for Interrogation, which to be follow'd by Imprisonment then Shooting as a Spy by Order of Dundee) while Simon Fraser whispers to the Chief, who nods, then resumes his wrothful Discourse. Whereat Simon Fraser returns to me and says in a low Voice: —Lord John Murray will speak with you directlie.

P.S. Of my Discourse with Lord John and my Journey to Dunkeld, I shall write anon; being presently compell'd to stay from Writing by reason I am so wearied and so sleepie.

* Highland robber. The term was sometimes used to denote a Highland clansman in his capacity of foot-soldier.

14.
‘ KILLY-CRANKIE ’

Castle Mingis,
27th/28th July, 1689.

I WRITE THIS Last Section of my Journall in Haste and Sorrow, within the Castle at Weem, where together with the poor remnant of MacKay's Army, Samuel and myself have presently taken Refuge from the Victorious (tho' now Leader-less) Highlanders. And I continue from my Meeting with Lord John Murray:

By and by, Lord John Murray dismisseth his Gentlemen in a Mightie Passion, they departing in a Huff, verie Haughty and murmuring 'mongst themselves. Whereafter he questions me verie close for the space of about half an hour concerning who I might be, and my Knowledge of the Campaign &c., I being verie Frank and holding nothing from him (saving that I am a Woman), as, perceiving Lord Murray belike to be an Ally sent by Heaven in this Hour of my Necessitie, 'twould be Follie to do other. (And I am encourag'd in this Belief by what both Colin Du and Samuel have reported to me concerning Lord Murray.)

—Well, Mr. Johnson, says he, —I will e'en trust you as you have trusted myself and will this verie Night, with a man of mine to guide you, send you to MacKay as Emissarie and you be willing.

—With all my Heart, I reply, and feel a bound of Hope. —MacKay is near at Hand? I ask.

Reply's he: —in an Express I receiv'd this Morning, MacKay tells me he marches to Dunkeld from Perth on the morrow.

(Whereat I rejoyce greatly for this meaneth that Samuel hath reach'd Colin Du with my Letters.)

—Dundee, you say doth purpose to pass by Struan ten days from when you saw him, (he continues). —Today is the 25th; Dundee then reaches Struan which is where you were imprison'd, on the Morrow. The Day appointed for the Clans' Assembling is the 29th, you say. This can only mean that the Gathering Place intended for the Clans is here at Blair Castle. And to think 'tis mine own Home!

I must have look'd something puzzl'd at this, for he hastens to explain, telling me Stewart of Ballechin (his own Steward!) hath upon Receipt of Orders from Dundee seiz'd the Castle for King James. Thus he, Murray, is presently constrain'd to besiege his own Seat with 1200 of his Clans-men.

—But the Insolent Caterans, (continues Murray), —do murmur and complain, demanding to know for what Cause they do this; I fear that and I were to tell 'em 'tis to take Blair for MacKay, they'd straightway declare for Dundee*.

And he charges me that I inform MacKay of his (Murray's) present Pass and that he is like to be compell'd to raise the Siege. Murray goes on to explain to me that the Cause whereby Dundee had come to Struan before was to persuade Lord John Murray to a Meeting, Lord John declining as he saw no Profit in coming together where both must disagree; I must suppose my being held

* Which is exactly what they did, the following morning! (see Footnote at end of Chapter 13.)

at Struan was against Dundee's coming to that Place, Dundee not staying at Glen Roy all that time.

And now Lord Murray waxeth mightie Eager, his Eyes flashing in his dark-complected Countenance, and exclaims that, and MacKay but strike now, he can be at Blair on the 27th, before one half of the Clans are assembled belike.

—And who holds Blair, holds Scotland, (he says), —Blair being the Key of the Kingdom as 'twere. —But now, Mr. Johnson, (says Lord Murray), —you shall dine and rest for a space before departing for Dunkeld while I prepare a Letter for MacKay.

And so it was that later that same evening, myself and a wild Highlandman who was to be my Guide departed from the Camp at Blair and setting our faces towards the South-east, began our Journey to Dunkeld. At first 'twas prettie easy Going what with there being a good enough Path by Garry-side and the Countrie in this Vale of Blair not overly Steep nor Broken. But by and by we are come to a most Fearfull Chasm where the Road became a Meer Ledge scratch'd along the side of a Horrid Precipice; and moreover it now waxing Dark, in part from the Lateness of the Hour, also because the Sheer Walls of the Defile suffer'd but little Light to penetrate therein, I become Fearfull lest I lose my Footing, for the Roaring of Garry in its Rockie Bed far below doth warn me that a Slip is Death. As we rest for a little Space I ask what this Place is and whether there be not a Safer Road to Dunkeld. He reply's the Place is call'd Rin Ruari and adds something scornfull (I give his verie words to show the Highlander's curious Usage of Speech), —Herself will be a verie Good Road whateffer.

At last we are come out of this Dreadfull Place and tho' the greater Part of our Journey (by Tummel and Tay) was yet to be accomplish'd, I esteem'd it Nothing, so great was my Joy to be quit of that Terrible Rin Ruari. And arriv'd in Dunkeld betimes in the Morning of the 26th of July, where my old Land-lord was verie pleased to see me and shew'd me to my Chamber where was all my Gear and Moneys Safe and Secure. I thank'd Murray's Fellow and offer'd him some Payment (I something Diffident as being uncertain if 'twould give Offence, he being a Highlander) which he took readily enow and so departed. On my inquiring was MacKay arriv'd? my Land-lord made reply he was not yet come but was departed Saint Johnston* (so 'twas bruited) and expected here this verie Day. So, after partaking of breakfast I did go to bed (being prettie wearie after my Night's Travelling), having charg'd my Land-lord that he wake me instanter upon MacKay's coming.

My Land-lord waking me I don the Suit of Clothes he doth provide (my own being quite wore out) and going into the Town do find many People abroad tho' the Hour be late, harkening to a distant Noise of Drums, and in a little space the Van of MacKay's Armie enters the Town. Now is there much Stir and Confusion as Companies are told off to their Quarters and Bivouacs, and I fear wearisome Delays before I can gain Audience with MacKay; but on my importuning an Officer of Leven's and saying I am sent by Murray, himself escorts me incontinent to a Commodious Dwelling on the outskirts of the Town, where after waiting for a little space in an outer Room I am sent for up. I am shewn into a Chamber where besides Aides and a Secretarie, is a Man of huge Stature in a Red Coat, large and square of Face, with a Look Hot and Impatient yet something puzzl'd withall as did put me in mind of a strong Bull or Bear in the Baiting-ring. This can be none other than the Commander-in-Chief of the

* Perth.

Convention's Forces, Viz, Lieutenant-Generall Hugh MacKay of Scourie, one-time Fellow-Campaigner with Dundee when they fought in the Dutch Service.

—Well, Mr. Johnson, (says he), I receiv'd your Intelligence through one Black Colin of Fortingall and so you see me in Dunkeld. And now you are come, I believe, with word from Lord John Murray.

And he holds his Hand out for the Letter. After reading which he begins pace up and down and the little Doubting Cast doth vanish from his Countenance, and he slaps the Beaver* in his Hand against his Thigh.

—I have him now! (he exclaims, communing with himself). —And Murray but hold the Pass until my Armie be through it, Blair Castle will be mine tomorrow.

—My Lord, if I might be so bold as to make an Observation? (I venture, something nettl'd that he hath made none Acknowledgement of my Service, saving that by Implication he hath acted on my Letter dispatch'd to Colin Du by the Hand of Samuel).

—And it be brief, Mr. Johnson, (he reply's something Curt and Impatient).

—My Lord, (I return), —'tis simply this: I would urge you have a Care concerning Dundee's Highland Host, who e'en now are belike beginning to arrive at Blair. When I saw them in Lochaber they appear'd to me verie Hardy and Fierce, such as would be a Terrible Foe in Battle. And consider this my Lord: to reach Blair you must first thread a Narrow Pass where an Ambuscade could maul your Troops. 'Tis doubtfull if Murray could prevent it for his Men are like to mutinie and declare for Dundee at any hour. But let us suppose you accomplish the Passage safelie; if the Highlanders attack you'd be compell'd to fight 'em on their own Ground, which being Steep and

* Hat.

Hillie doth give 'em Vantage. I urge you, My Lord, that you let 'em have Blair for the Present. Then, and you but wait, the Highlanders will disperse soon enow, for they lack Provision having tasted neither Bread nor Salt for weeks, and besides their Nature will not suffer 'em to wait o'erlong. And you try Conclusions with 'em now My Lord, I own I would not place a Wager on your Winning.

MacKay stares at me as one who doubts he has heard aright. —In this Letter, (he declares), —Murray says the Day of the Clans' Assembling is the 29th; which Matter you inform'd him of yourself, Murray says. Today is but the 26th. And we reach Blair tomorrow, think you that more than half the Clans will be gather'd there? You said in your Report, Mr. Johnson, they number'd 4000 in Toto; so we'd be contending with but 2000 at the most. Know you my Strength? 'Tis 4000 Foot besides two Corps of Horse!

And, smiling like to a Boy who proudly counts his little Store of Toy Soldiers, he tells off on his Fingers: —MacKay's, Balfour's, Ramsay's, Buchan's, Kenmure's, Leven's, Hasting's, Belhaven's Horse, Annandale's Horse.

And he goes on to say contemptuously: —What can a Rabble of starving Caterans accomplish 'gainst a Disciplin'd and well-Fed Armie twice their Strength? (And smiles on me as to say, See how Baseless your Fears are!)

Perceiving it were but Vain Follie to press further Argument upon this Man, I inquire of him what I should now do, my Dutie as prescrib'd by the Doctor and Fletcher being presently accomplish'd. Whereat MacKay says I am to accompany the Armie as Intelligencer (whatsoever that might signify!).

—May I join with Belhaven's Horse? (I ask), —for I know the Gentleman and would gladly serve with him, and besides I have a Nag stabl'd in the Town.

Which Request is deny'd me, MacKay declaring I must

accompany his own Regiment, and to present myself at four o' clock in the morning and to leave my Nag behind.

And being dismiss'd, I sought out my Lord Belhaven at his Billet, who tho' Busy with a Thousand Cares welcom'd me most graciously (rememb'ring me from our Sojourn in Haddingtonshire) and press'd me to sup with him. As we did eat, I made Inquirie concerning Samuel to which he reply'd that he'd heard there was a Blackamoor Lad presently a-serving with the Sutlers, and gives me a Note requesting he be transferr'd to my Service, and will stand Suretie for such Accomodation.

Taking my leave, I begin searching among the Rows of Tents on the Haugh by the ruin'd Gothick Church, and by and by am directed to the Sutlers' Lines where I find Samuel. Follows a Joyfull Re-Union with my Young Friend, whom I take back to my Lodgings (his Master mightie Sullen but durst not gainsay my Lord Belhaven's Command). And Samuel gives me back my Journall which he hath guarded all this time, and while he sleeps I do write it up Compleat until the time of my arriving at Blair; also Letters to Fletcher and the Doctor concerning the News from Athole, these to be dispatch'd by my Land-lord on the Morrow by the Hand of one he knows. At which point I am constrain'd by Wearinesse to leave off Writing and to take some Rest.

Up verie betimes, and taking my Measuring-Staff (and my Journall in my Pocket) I go with Samuel to the Mustering-Place which is the Haughs beside the Church, where to Tuck of drum the Armie doth form up by Companies each in their Severall Regiments. And by First Light on the 27th of July (it being Saturday) the Armie sets out at a brisk pace, the Men a-singing *Lilliburlero* and *The Lowlands of Holland*, and by ten o' clock is arriv'd by way of Moulen at the Mouth of that Dread Defile, Rin Ruari (which I hear the Soldiers to call Killy-crankie).

Strange to say, the Place doth appear even more Horrible by Day than by Night, for now are its Terrors no longer cloak'd by Darknesse but in Plain Sight. Here the Armie halted for the space of two hours, until Noon.

As the Soldiers gratefullie settl'd themselves down to wait, I observ'd the Scene: the Fusileers, Edinburgh and Hasting's Regiments* in Scarlett; Balfour's, Buchan's and Ramsay's in the Liverie of the Scots in the Dutch Service; the Horse in Coats of Yellow Buff and Steel Caps, their Officers with long Periwigs a-falling from below broad-brimm'd Beavers onto shining Back-and-Breasts; the Bells of Arms glitt'ring in the Sun. 'Twas as Brave and Gallant a Sight as you could wish to see; but to the fore loom'd the Dark and Gloomie Mountains of Athole, split asunder by that Terrific Defile, the Pass of KILLY-CRANKIE.

—'Tis bruited, Sir, that Murray hath abandon'd Blair and did join with us at Moulen; and that Colonel Lauder hath been despatch'd in Murray's Room, and with two hundred Fusileers holds the Head of the Pass 'gainst our Coming, (says Samuel, who looks with some Concern upon its Entrance).

—I pray 'tis so, (I rejoin), —for 'tis as nigh perfect a Spot for Ambuscade as the Enemy could wish for.

— Be you afraid, Sir?, asks Samuel as one seeking Re-Assurance.

—Aye, that I am, Boy, I reply, —and so I daresay are everie one of these four thousand, tho' they hide it well enough. And he which fears not in such a Pass is but a Fool, for Fear, and it mastereth us not, makes us to be Prudent and Wise in Danger that we preserve Life and Limb. (Which Remark seem'd to comfort the Lad somewhat.)

But now the Drums beat and the Bugles ring and the

* See Notes for alternative names of some of the Regiments.

Bells of Arms are un-pil'd, then the Armie marches forward, its Ranks contracting to a Double File as it steps out upon that Narrow Path I'd travell'd but two Nights before. And now it waxeth Dark as the Walls of the Defile close around us, and the Roaring of the River dins in our Ears, and the only other Sounds to be heard are the shuffling of thousands of Feet and the Jingle of Horses' Harness, the Soldiers being fall'n strangely Silent so Heavy are their Spirits by Reason of their Horrible Surroundings. I look upon the Birch-trees clothing the far Bank, and in my mind I see hundreds of Men hid in Ambush, and the Musket-stocks settling 'gainst Shoulders, and Fingers beginning to press on Triggers. And as my Fancie thus spins its Web of Apprehension, there comes upon a sudden a Distant Report, and away to the fore a Trooper cries out and sways in the Saddle, then he falls. I shrink, convinc'd a Storm of Bullets is about to burst amongst us, and I daresay everie Man in the Armie thinks the same; but there comes no other Shot, and the Column continues on its Way without further Scathe.

But now the Sheer Sides of the Gorge begin to draw back and the Sun can now be seen again and the Roaring of the Pent-in River lessens; so we are come out of the Pass of Killy-crankie and into the Wider Valley beyond where all is Emptinesse and Light and Silence. Now the Armie stands to Arms; away to the Fore I can see Mounted Scouts a-galloping up the Vale of Blair, perforce to seek Intelligence of Dundee. And in a little space back they come, and by and by the Bruit spreads that Dundee's Van approaches down the Valley. Then one comes from MacKay saying the Generall would see me. Bidding Samuel accompany me, I go with the Soldier to where the Generall sits his Horse.

—Well, Mr. Intelligencer, (says he, smiling as one who hath accomplish'd a Pettie Victorie over another), —

where are your Fears now! The Pass is safelie behind us and the Enemy to the Fore. They come as Sheep for the Slaughter; in this Broad and Level Place we'll cut 'em to Pieces. But perchance we have o'erlook'd something, (he continues in Ironie), —and you have further Wise Counsell for our Ears before Battle is join'd?

—And it please Your Lordship, (I return), —would it not be wise to make Assurance doubly Sure? If we were to ascend yonder Rising Ground we'd see their Dispositions the more plain.

Whereat MacKay smiles as one who indulges a Foolish Child and makes reply: —Why, if that be your Pleasure, Mr. Intelligence, let us e'en go and see.

And in a little space we are come to the Summitt of an Acclivity whence can be seen, a short Mile up the Valley, small Parties of the Enemy advancing. Whereat MacKay shakes his Head at me, (as to say, You see, Mr. Johnson), and sends one of the Aides he has with him, back with Word to advance the Foot.

Yet I am uneasie, believing Dundee to be more Subtil than this, and suspect some Ruse. Then I feel Samuel a-tugging of my Sleeve and look to where he points to the Right. And see a Highland Armie a-coming down the Hillside upon us!

I shew MacKay; for a moment he stares astonied, then with a Curse wheels his Horse about and follow'd by his Aides, gallops back towards his Imperill'd Troops.

When Samuel and I reach the Armie again it is toiling up the Hillside to their Right. I perceive MacKay's Intent which is to win to the Ridge atop the Hillside before Dundee can reach there. But when we are arriv'd at the Top, Lo! (in the Manner of the Highland Countrie) 'tis not the Summit after all, for beyond it is a further Rise and atop that Rise is Dundee's Armie!

Plainlie Dundee intends no Sudden Attack, for his Host disposes itself in Battle Order without any Haste. As well they might, for even I who have never been a-Campaigning (save in my Plays and Stories) could tell MacKay was in a Sorry Pass, having nothing to do but extend his Armie that it cross the Plain atop the Ridge from side to side, to the end it be not outflank'd. Which Manoeuvre was accomplish'd (as I could plainly see, MacKay's Regiment being on the Right and higher than the Rest) at Sore Cost; MacKay's Armie being now stretch'd out in a long thin Ribband but three Men deep, with a Gap in the Centre betwixt Kenmure's and Leven's, and to the Rear, covering the Gap, Belhaven's and Annandale's Horse. I could not but admire how Dundee had turn'd the Tables on MacKay, whose Troops were now extended in a perilouslie thin Line, with the Highlanders above 'em, and behind 'em a slope down to Garry and Escape thorough the Pass block'd, by Reason of the Vast Multitude of Baggage-Animals. 'Twas Ironicall to reflect that the Highland Armie was led by Dundee a Lowlander, and the Lowland Armie led by MacKay a Highlander!

Now is there Naught to do but wait. Dundee's Armie being in Plain Sight above us, 'tis clear what he intends. His Numbers being much the less compar'd to ours, he is constrain'd to leave large Gaps between the Clans to the End that he cover MacKay's Line. And that his Men be not dazzl'd by the Sun as they advance (for, holding the Higher Ground 'tis they which must attack), 'tis plain he purposes to hold 'em back, – no easie task with Highlanders, until the Sun be gone down. And now beginneth a Sillie Game according to the Curious Custom of these Modern Times, Viz, a Contemplation of the Enemy by both Sides (to what End I know not save it be peradventure to stiffen Resolve or concentrate the Mind upon the Tremendous Matters impending), and is accompanied by a Discharge of Musketrie which can effect no Hurt at all by Reason of the Distance, also some Popping from MacKay's three Field-Pieces, Pitifull little Leathern Tubes which can scarce cast a Ball to the Enemy Lines, and are named in Mockerie, Dear Sandy's Stoups.

Dundee's own Troop of Horse, being on the Left of their Line, is straight opposite MacKay's Regiment, so I can see Dundee plain, Brave in his Scarlett Coat, which however by and by he exchanges for one of Buff (as being I daresay more Serviceable and the less Conspicuous), but from time to time he leaves his Troop to mingle with the Clans, belike to encourage 'em with Chearfull Words.

Being near to MacKay (for in Spite of his seeming Contempt for my Opinion, he hath commanded me to stay close), I observe him to point towards the Camerons and hear him say to a young Officer of the Scots Fusileers:

—See over there, your Father, Sir Ewen Cameron of Lochiel with his Wild Savages. Would you rather be with him?

To which the Officer made Disdainfull Reply: —'tis no Matter, My Lord, what I would like, but have a Care, for those Savages may be nearer you tonight than you would wish.

But now the Sun, which hath seem'd at times this long afternoon, to have stood still in the Heavens, begins to drop fast as it doth when nearing the Horizon. My Bowels churn and 'tis difficult I find to draw Breath, but for the sake of Samuel who stands beside me, I smile as chearfullie as I may, and make some Foolish Jest, I disremember what. Charging my Piece with one of Sir Isaac's Ridiculous Silvern Bullets, I pump up the Chamber with Air. All along the Line, Orders ring out as MacKay's Troops prepare to receive the Enemy:

—Musketeers, Musketeers have a Care! —Prime your

Pans! —Open your Charges! —Charge with Powder! —Charge with Bullet! —Ram Home! —Withdraw your Scourers! —Cock your Musketts!

And now the Sun is falling fast; as it dips below the Mountains, there bursts from the Highlanders a Wild, Long, Triumphant Cheer, which is answer'd by such a Feeble and Spirit-less Shout from our own Men, that I know at once with a Thrill of Horror that the Terrifying Sight of their un-Familiar and Ferocious Foe hath unmann'd 'em, that their Courage fails.

Dundee now gives the Signall; casting aside their Plaids the Clans-men advance, slowlie at the first, then faster as they move from the slope to the level, dropping now in Scores as the Volleys of Musketrie from the Lowland Troops crash out ever and again. Yet still they come, never firing a Shot, thorough the Smoak of that Terrible Musketrie, until they be nearlie upon our Line. Then, discharging their own Musketts all together in one Appalling Thunderclap of Sound, they draw their Broadswords and yelling, rush wildly upon our Line, while our Musketeers struggle to fix their Bayonetts in the Muzzles of their Firelocks.

MacKay's being not as yet engag'd, I can witness the Scene below me: Hacking with their Terrible Swords the Clans-men close with the Lowlanders and for a little space there's Silence, save for the Clash of Swordplay and the Cursing of Men. Such Horrid Sights as I now did witness will ever affright me in my Dreams: Skulls cleft asunder that the Brains fly out; Limbs lopped clean through — Blood from the sever'd Stumps thereof jetting forth like Scarlett Fountains.

Then the Clans burst through our Line as a Keen Axe drives through Rotten Timber, and everywhere our Men scatter and flee — I see Balfour's, now Lauder's Fusileers, and over there half Ramsay's break and run; now they're swept in a Confus'd and Struggling Mass down into the Garry by a Screaming Wave of Highlanders. 'Tis all but over; in a Twinkling MacKay's Armie hath vanish'd, save for little Clumps of the more Resolute or Fortunate, that stand here and there like Islands in a Raging Sea. There's my Lord Belhaven gallantlie essaying to rally his Troopers; but in Vain, they turn and gallop off the Stricken Field. And far down the Pass comes back the Echoes of Flying Troops battling to escape, and the Exulting Yells of the Pursuing Highlanders.

See over there, Dundee at the head of his Troop charges a remnant of our Horse which scatters and flees. Now he wheels his Troop, and perceiving MacKay's yet standing, gallops towards us in a Headlong Furious Charge. Around me the Soldiers raise their Musketts and fire, but Fear hath them so in Thrall their Bullets for the most part fly wild. The Sight of that line of glitt'ring Blades and Flying Hoofs sweeping down upon 'em is too much for their overtested Courage to endure; first one then another drops his Firelock and turns to flee, then in a trice all turn Tail with Cries of Terror and run. MacKay, to his credit, chases after, striking at 'em with the Flat of his Sword and cursing 'em for Vile Cowards, in a Vain Attempt to rally them. (For myself, tho' terrify'd, I've stood my Ground and have prevail'd upon Samuel to do likewise, knowing 'tis the Safer Part, for to flee a Stricken Field is to be pursu'd and slain. We crouch low 'gainst the Ground hoping thus perchance to avoid being observ'd.)

Now Dundee, reining in verie near to where we lie, doth pause awhile to look around the Victorious Field. And perceiving Hasting's yet un-broke, raises his Sword-arm to wave on his Troop to the Attack. And I, seeing my Lord Dundee, so Gallant and Brave in his moment of Triumph as he stands in the Stirrups, his Sword lifted high, a smile upon his Comelie face - every Part of me is fill'd with Admiration, yea, and Love.

Then Samuel, gesturing with his chin toward Dundee, doth bend upon me a Look all Keen and Urgent as to say: see, Fate hath deliver'd you this chance! But – to slay the Man that hath ensnar'd my Heart? All my Being recoils in Horror from the thought, 'tho sensible that 'tis my plain Dutie. But in that Moment I know the Thing that I must do and it seems to me that 'tis my Fate I should accomplish this. I take Aim at that Vulnerable Mark below his uprais'd Arm. I shoot: Dundee reels in the Saddle; one of his Officers hastens to his Side and catching him in his arms, bears him gently to the Ground. They kneel around their fall'n Leader, and in a little space draw a Plaid over him that it hides his Countenance. By which I know Dundee is Dead.

As to what happen'd immediately thereafter I have no Remembrance save in Generall, being sunk in a Stupor of Horror and Miserie; Samuel must perforce have made shift to lay hold of two riderless Nags, for when I came to myself we were riding through a Broken Waste of Hills and Mosses, it then being full Night and our way trending to the South-ward as I could tell by the Stars. And arriving at Weem a little before the Middle of the Night we do seek Refuge in Castle Mingis (which is Friendlie to our Cause) finding it full of MacKay's Soldiers which have escap'd the Rout. Having taken a Fall, I am sore Hurt inside and perforce must bide here at Weem, and the Highlanders come or no.

And so I make Haste to bring this my Journall to a Conclusion, it being Pain and Sorrow for me to write, for tho' I've done my Dutie I believe, my Heart is broke in the Fulfilling thereof.

And now, Farewell, Kind Friends which read this, for I think 'twill not be long before I travell to that Bourne whither Dundee hath gone before me. (And my Hope and

Comfort must be this: that in that Place where is no Strife, nor Tears nor any kind of Hurt, but only Joy and Love, we may perchance meet again.) There, 'tis done, and I give my Journall to Samuel that hath promis'd to see it safe deliver'd to Fletcher.

—o-o-o—

Transcribed by: Ross Laidlaw, East Lothian

POSTSCRIPT

What happened to Aphra Behn? Did she die of a broken heart and internal injuries shortly after arriving at Castle Menzies? Or did she perhaps recover, and spend the remainder of her days living incognito in Scotland? (If she survived, I don't think she returned to London, where she was too well-known for some record of her re-appearance not to have come down to us.)

Perhaps her final resting-place is in the Kirkyard at Saltoun (the parish of Fletcher and Burnet) or in the Maitland Vault at St.Mary's Haddington, beside Richard Maitland to whom she dedicated her novel ***Oroonoko***. So far, I have been unable to discover any answers. But one lives in hope; perhaps diligent search among the Fletcher Papers in the National Library of Scotland will one day unearth a document which will tell us that ...

R.L.

NOTES

1. ‘ A HARD TEST ’

‘Astrea’s pen’

‘Astrea’ was Aphra Behn’s pseudonym among her friends and admirers. Contemporaries also refer to her as ‘Sappho’ — not always in a favourable context.

‘the Woman damns the Poet’

A quotation from the Preface to her play ***The Lucky Chance***. In the Preface she argues passionately that women should have as much freedom as men to write about sex and other topics then regarded as the preserve of male writers.

‘most ador’d Mazarine’

This was Hortense Mancini, Duchess of Mazarine — a bisexual adventuress for whom Aphra Behn developed a passionate ‘crush’, and to whom in 1688 she dedicated her story ***The History of the Nun***.

‘Honest Hoyle’

John Hoyle, a lawyer, was an atheist and bisexual with whom Aphra Behn had a passionate affair in the 1670’s. Although bitterly hurt by his desertion of her c. 1677, she remained friends with him. ‘Honest’ surely indicates that their relationship was now that of friends, rather than lovers.

‘censur’d some of my Plays... as being Licentious’

In 1682 Burnet wrote a letter to the poetess Anne Wharton, in which he refers to Aphra Behn as, ‘so abominably vile a woman, and rallies not only all religion but all virtue in so odious and obscene a manner’. Anne Wharton (whose husband wrote the words to Purcell’s tune of ***Lilliburllero***) revealed the contents of the letter to Aphra Behn, who is probably here referring to the above passage.

'a new Dramatick Work by Mr. Tate'

This can surely only refer to Purcell's ***Dido and Aeneas***, the first true English opera. It was performed at Josias Priest's 'School for Young Gentlewomen' in Chelsea for the first time, probably in December 1689.

'Poem to Queen Mary'

This was ***A Congratulatory Poem to ... Queen Mary upon Her Arrival in England***. It was written very soon after the Proclamation of William and Mary on February 13th 1689. In the poem, Aphra Behn tells how she is persuaded to accept Mary as Queen because she is the daughter of James II ('Great Lord of all my Vows'); she pointedly omits any reference to William. Burnet's visit is recorded in ***A Pindaric Poem to the Reverend Doctor Burnet on the honour he did me of enquiring after me and my muse*** – her last work (that is, before the discovery of her Journal).

'Mr. Kemp'

'Mr. and Mrs. Kemp' were the code-names for James VII and II and his Queen, Mary of Modena. Devised by Scot and Covenanter, James Johnston, they were used by William of Orange's Intelligence Service in the build-up to the Glorious Revolution.

'Lord Dundee'

John Graham of Claverhouse (the 'Bluidy Clavers' of legend) was created Viscount Dundee by James II on the 12th November 1688.

'that they choose James above the Prince'

The Convention of the Estates summoned by circular letter from William of Orange, was virtually an ***ad hoc*** Parliament. Its purpose, Scotland being still then an independent nation with its own Parliament, was to decide who should reign in Scotland – James or William. As the Convention was overwhelmingly Whig and Presbyterian in composition, the scales were heavily weighted in William's favour. Colin Lindsay, Earl of Balcarres, and

MacKenzie the Lord Advocate were old and staunch friends of Dundee. (Balcarres had accompanied Claverhouse and the army of Scotland south to support James, in face of the threat of invasion by William. They were almost alone among those who remained loyal to James; in February 1689, with a few faithful troopers, they returned to Scotland. MacKenzie also earned the soubriquet 'Bluidy' for his brisk treatment of Covenanter prisoners after Bothwell Brig, at which battle Claverhouse was present.)

'as many Elephants as Jacobites'

Burnet is paraphrasing a remark of Dundee's, made at a time when he was responsible for maintaining law and order in the Covenanting South West of Scotland, that there were 'as many elephants as loyalists in Galloway'.

'by... Experience... fitted to play this Part'

By the direct order of Charles II, Aphra Behn had been sent as a spy to Antwerp during the Anglo-Dutch War. Had a Report sent by her to the government not been ignored, the Dutch attack on the Thames-Medway might have been foiled.

'his daughter Anne flaunts Orange Knacks'

Anne (later Queen Anne) was seen at the theatre with Lady Churchill both sporting orange ribbons.

'my old sicknesse'

In 1686 Aphra Behn fell ill of what was variously described at the time as 'the pox', gout and sciatica, and may have been a form of arthritis. Her physical ill-health must have been compounded by: the loss of John Hoyle as a lover – a blow from which she never really recovered, her unrequited passion for Hortense Mancini, the relentless pressure to write to keep the wolf from the door, and the political thunderclouds gathering above her old patron James II to whom she showed unswerving loyalty. From this point in her life, references in her writings to herself as 'dying', or 'near to a tomb' suggest that her bouts of illness struck with increasing frequency and severity.

2. 'A PHILOSOPHICKALL ENGINE '

'my Death... (and) Funerall'

Gilbert Burnet's plan was duly carried out, Aphra Behn's 'death' being announced on April 16th, and her 'funeral' in Westminster Abbey taking place on the 20th – a task well within the capabilities of a resourceful schemer like Burnet.

'Andrew Fletcher of Saltoun'

Born in 1653 to Sir Andrew Fletcher of Saltoun in Haddingtonshire and Catherine Bruce (a descendant of Robert de Bruce), young Andrew Fletcher was tutored by Gilbert Burnet (see Appendix) for four years from the age of twelve. In 1678, after some years of travel on the Continent, he is sent to the Convention of the Estates of Scotland as a member for Haddingtonshire. During the next few years he shows his courage, unselfish stance on matters of principle, and 'republicanism', by boldly standing up to first Lauderdale, then the Duke of York (later James II) in their capacity of Secretary of State for Scotland, on occasions when their regimes smacked of absolutism. So hot in fact did he make Scotland for himself, that he was forced to flee first to England, then abroad. In 1685, out of principle, he joined Monmouth's Rebellion, although he expected it to fail. Fortunately for Fletcher, his shooting of the Mayor of Taunton as a result of a quarrel, forced him to flee abroad once more and thus avoid the consequences of Sedgemoor. He was on board William's invasion fleet of 1688 (as was his old tutor Burnet), and returned to Scotland, where he was soon re-possessed of his Saltoun estates (forfeited after Sedgemoor). Although unaccountably excluded from the all-important Convention of 1689, he followed its proceedings with passionate interest. Denied an active role in the Convention, he became a leading member of 'The Club' – a political pressure group which effectively controlled the Convention and tried (unsuccessfully) to curb the prerogatives of the new monarch. Outraged by Glencoe, and disillusioned by English sabotaging tactics against the Darien Scheme, Fletcher became increasingly critical of William's policy regarding Scotland, and bitterly opposed the moves towards Union, which he predicted would obliterate Scotland's independence and erode her national identity. After the Union (pushed through against the national will by 'a parcel of rogues in a nation'), Fletcher retired from public life, disillusioned but until his death (in 1716) deeply 'concerned for the ruin of his country'. If he could re-visit Scotland today, he would probably be heartened to find the Cause for which he fought so passionately, more alive perhaps than at any time since his own, and showing signs of a prospect of ultimate success.

'Hamilton of Biel'

John Hamilton, Lord Belhaven, was an almost exact contemporary of Fletcher and shared his hostility towards the Union. (His moving speech against the Union – delivered in the last Scottish Parliament, can still be read). At Killiecrankie, he commanded a corps of cavalry – 'Belhaven's Horse', in MacKay's army; he is said to have behaved gallantly during the battle, although unable to prevent the flight of his troopers.

'Mr. Foe a youngish Gentleman'

From the details which Aphra Behn gives, it is clear that this is Daniel Defoe (plain Foe before c. 1695), author of ***Robinson Crusoe***; at the time of her meeting with him, he would be aged twenty nine. In his action-packed and colourful career, Defoe was: 'out' with Monmouth, a business entrepreneur (twice bankrupted), a prolific writer on a wide variety of topics (politics, crime, religion, psychology, the supernatural etc., etc.), arrested several times and imprisoned (plus a stint in the pillory) for his political views, a secret agent in England and Scotland. In several respects his career shows remarkable parallels with Aphra Behn's! Defoe's hostile views concerning Dundee were probably coloured by his own Dissenting background. This made him a natural sympathizer with the Covenanters who have been portrayed as persecuted martyrs in his ***Memoirs of the Church of Scotland***, (London, 1717), and in Wodrow's ***History of the Sufferings of the Church of Scotland***, (2 vols., Edinburgh 1721-1722), etc.

'A Conceal'd Weapon'

The action of the air gun described by Aphra Behn sounds similar to that of an air gun of Queen Kristina of Sweden (1644-1654) made by Hans Koler of Kitzing, featuring a reservoir which had to be pumped full of air. The earliest examples of air guns are of this type; ones using a spring-operated plunger appeared rather later.

P.S. The existence of a popular belief that Dundee was in league with the Devil is confirmed by Scott in a Note to Chapter 16 of his ***Old Mortality***:

'Proof against Shot given by Satan.

The belief of the Covenanters that... Claverhouse had obtained from the Devil a charm which rendered him proof against leaden bullets...'

And in another Note:

'... the many extraordinary traditions current in Scotland concerning Claverhouse's famous black charger, which was generally believed to have been a gift to its rider from the Author of Evil... This horse...and its rider...are said to have outstripped and...turned, a hare upon the Bran-Law, near the head of Moffat Water, where the descent is so precipitous, that no merely earthly horse could keep its feet, or merely mortal rider could keep the saddle.'

'O Intwin'd Extasies'

Whether this implies full lesbian intercourse or merely 'heavy petting' is uncertain. What is certain is the growing ambiguity of Aphra Behn's sexual feelings towards the end of her life, accentuated perhaps by her traumatic affair with the bisexual John Hoyle. Witness the poem she quotes, 'To the fair Clarinda who made love to me', also her Dedication (to Hortense Mancini) of ***The History of the Nun***, where she declares 'how infinitely one of your own sex ador'd you' and says that of all her conquests 'your Grace had not subdu'd a more entire slave', and a poem by her (which appeared posthumously in Gildon's ***Miscellany*** of 1692) describing a useless visit to the country to try to cure herself of love for 'a fair lady' – 'the lovely charmer' who has made of her 'a wretched conquest'. Steamy stuff! But perhaps, in view of recent government legislation, it may not be 'prudent to inquire' (to quote Aphra Behn) too deeply into her love life.

3. ' A LOW THIN MAN, EYES FULL OF FIRE '

'a Mr. Wm. Carstares'

Carstares (nicknamed 'Cardinal Carstares' by his rivals) along with Gilbert Burnet one of the architects of the Glorious Revolution, was the trusted confidential secretary of William of Orange and one of the chief agents in his intelligence service. Earlier, he had been arrested in 1674 for distributing pamphlets hostile to the Cabal – especially Lauderdale; and was subsequently imprisoned and tortured in Edinburgh Castle, for being implicated in the Rye House Plot, by which time he was secretly working for William. Both men were with William when he landed at Torbay and both had leading roles in establishing the new regime. Carstares was largely instrumental in establishing the Presbyterian, formerly persecuted, Church of the Covenanters as the National Kirk of Scotland. (Ironically, he was presented with the very thumbscrews used on him, as a memento!)

'the Duke of Hamilton (who is like to become the President of the Convention)'

William, 3rd Duke of Hamilton, did in fact become the President of the Convention. Carstares' strictures (which would with more justification be applicable to the 4th Duke) seem a little harsh. They may in fact mean no more than that Hamilton was big enough to change his mind when convinced he was wrong (as happened in 1692 when a rebuke in a letter from Fletcher persuaded him to 'assist in council'), and that he refused to truckle to William, preferring to keep an open mind as to the respective merits of William and James regarding which of them it would be better for Scotland to have as King.

'John Dalrymple, the Earl Stair'

In this case, Carstares' judgement would seem entirely appropriate. Dalrymple was the scheming and unscrupulous time-server who masterminded the Massacre of Glencoe, and the Act of Union.

'a vast ancient Church sadly ruin'd'

Happily, this is no longer the case; St. Mary's Haddington, partly destroyed by the English in the reign of Edward VI during the Siege of Haddington, was splendidly restored in the 1970's. On a plaque in the Lauderdale Aisle (the 'Chappel... of the Maitlands' which Aphra Behn mentions) is recorded the name of Richard Maitland to whom she dedicated ***Oroonoko***.

'Yester... where is a verie splendid Park'

Descendants of the Earl cherished and improved the heritage bequeathed to them, and today Yester is one of the glories of East Lothian.

'a Noble Pile of no vast antiquitie'

The building that Aphra Behn saw has been largely swallowed up in an early 19th century reconstruction in 'Waverly Gothic' style. In the 18th century the village of West Saltoun became a thriving community thanks to the enterprise of the Fletcher family, who introduced the manufacture of Holland cloth and pot barley to Scotland. The descendants of the Fletchers today still live on the estate, in the converted Stables; the Hall itself is divided into flats. A link with Gilbert Burnet is the Bishop Burnett Bequest of 1712, providing a yearly sum to be distributed among the poor and to augment the Burnett Library, and which is still administered by the parish minister.

'Ways and Means they should hear and weigh his Counsell'

Ways and means he found indeed, through the pressure group which he helped to establish – 'the Club'. (See Note on Andrew Fletcher, for Chapter 2.)

'a new book call'd The Scots Gardener'

Originally published in 1683, it has recently been reprinted.

'did the Scots scruple to put him aside?'

Fletcher is bending History slightly in the interests of his argument. It was actually Edward I of England who put aside his puppet Balliol, after that unhappy monarch had been driven at last to defy him.

'a ridge nam'd Falside Hill from the Castle there'

Fawside Castle was burnt (with its inhabitants) by the English in reprisal for resistance during the Battle of Pinkie in 1547. Rebuilt, it burned down accidentally in 1680 and for three centuries remained a roofless shell. It has recently been splendidly restored by one Tom King.

'he reply'd... that 'twas a Serf-Collar'

By an Act of the Scottish Parliament of 1606 coal-miners became Serfs; incredibly, this iniquitous legislation was not repealed until 1799!

'out with Argyll in the late Rebellion'

The original strategy for Monmouth's Rebellion was a two-pronged simultaneous attack – by Monmouth in the South-west of England, and by Archibald Campbell the Earl of Argyll in the West of Scotland. In the event, Argyll set sail on the 2nd May 1685 – several weeks earlier than Monmouth, who was delayed by lack of money and adverse weather. Lack of preparation, divided consels, and a lukewarm response all militated against the success of Argyll's venture. Many of his influential clansmen were skilfully detained in Edinburgh, so that less than half the full fighting strength of Clan Campbell joined their Chief, 'Mac Cailein Mor'. With the capture of his arms store, Argyll lost hope and courage and the enterprise disintegrated. He was captured fleeing in disguise, and executed as a traitor.

'a Nice Point of Law'

Fletcher's observation is reinforced by Smout, who cites the following: 'In 1770 a West India negro brought to Fife as a slave by a returned colonial adventurer applied to the Court of Session for his liberty, his case being supported by... the local colliers... His master died, however, before a decision was reached, and thus ended what had obviously been regarded as a test case applicable not merely to negro slavery in Scotland. In 1772 a decision of the English courts ruled that on English soil no man could be deemed a slave.'

'the hero of my book *Oroonoko*'

Published in 1688, ***Oroonoko*** tells the story of the life and horrifying death of an African Prince of noble character, captured and sold into slavery in Surinam, then an English colony. Aphra Behn claims that it is a true story, based on personal knowledge. (She maintains that she met and made friends with Oroonoko when she lived in Surinam for a short period in her twenties.) The book is remarkable for its complete absence of racial prejudice, and for its moving portrayal of courage and nobility of spirit in the face of terrible adversity. It has an arguable claim to be the first true novel in English, pre-dating by many years the works of Defoe, Fielding, Richardson and Smollett in that field.

'entering into the Citie'

Some authorities have suggested that Fletcher accompanied his friend Lord Belhaven to Edinburgh incognito, in the guise of Lord Belhaven's groom and bodyguard. Perhaps this mistake arose thus: Aphra Behn (dressed in the 'common black' of a servant or tradesman) was observed in the company of each gentleman on separate occasions en route to Edinburgh, and this gives rise to a confused report.

4. '... GRANT WARRANT TO REQUIRE HIM TO REMOVE OUT OF THE SAID CASTLE...'

'Fletcher stays with friends in the Cow-Gate'

Today, such an address could prove a social handicap; in 17th century Edinburgh, it was ***the*** place to live.

'my old friend and Benefactor Sir Thos. Gower'

Sir Thomas Gower stands as a kind of keystone in Aphra Behn's life. Through him she met many of the important people in her life, including her lover John Hoyle, and James, later to be King of England. Through him too, she was sent as a spy to Antwerp.

'Hackston of Rathillet'

The leader of the party which stopped the coach of Archbishop Sharp on the Magus Muir in Fife and murdered the prelate before his daughter's eyes. This event – the first in the Covenanting Rebellion of 1679, was followed by the defeat of Claverhouse's Dragoons at Drumclog by a large party of armed Covenanters. Fired by this success, the Covenanters raised an army from among their own numbers but were defeated by the Duke of Monmouth at Bothwell Brig, Claverhouse also being present at the battle. (These events are stirringly described by Scott in his novel ***Old Mortality***.)

P.S. The verb 'to Rathillet' seems to have started something of a vogue – 'to Glencoe' – to liquidate (1692); 'to Bowdlerize' – to expurgate (1818); 'Burke' – to murder (1829); 'to Maffick' – to celebrate riotously, from Mafeking (1900); and, a contribution from the Nazis, 'to Coventrate' – to obliterate (1940).

'And now is the Castle quite block'd up and invested'

It was to remain 'block'd up' for almost exactly three months, finally surrendering on 14th June. In the interim: to help in the blockade, the Cameronian Regiment was raised from the followers of Richard Cameron, a fanatical Covenanter who in 1680 had personally declared war on

Charles II (!); the Edinburgh Regiment – later the K.O.S.B. was raised; two bombardments were commenced from the south-west by General MacKay who arrived at Leith on 25th March; more batteries started up bombardments of mortar-bombs from near the Calton and from George Heriot's School on 6th April; on 4th June showers of hand-grenades fired from mortars descended on the Castle – these proving especially lethal; throughout the period bloody sallies and counter-sallies were made from and against the trenches dug by the besiegers around the western and northern approaches to the Castle. Following the surrender, Gordon was released on parole. After a peaceful retirement, he died in 1716.

5. '... THE LORD VISCOUNT DUNDEE HAD A CONFERENCE WITH THE DUKE OF GORDON AT THE POSTERN GATE OF THE CASTLE...'

'a Plot to murther him and Sir Geo. MacKenzie both'

Dundee had excellent reasons for his suspicions. As Public Enemy Number One (at least to the majority Whig Party) who had managed against all the odds to persuade Gordon to continue holding Edinburgh Castle, and who was an obvious rallying-point for a Jacobite Opposition, it would be extremely convenient if something were to happen to Dundee. (One can just imagine Dalrymple 'putting out a Contract on' Dundee.) The Convention's reaction to Dundee's complaint, as reported by Aphra Behn, is confirmed by Dundee's friend Colin Balcarres, in his 'Memoirs'.

'Dundee is today departed out of the Citie'

Dundee's famous ride out of Edinburgh is commemorated in Sir Walter Scott's well-known verses on 'Bonnie Dundee'. Aphra Behn's description of Dundee's appearance accords closely with the portrait of Claverhouse by an unknown artist, in the Scottish National Portrait Gallery in Edinburgh.

'a Stratagem to stir up the Populace against the Jacobites'

Hamilton's ruse seems to have been highly successful. As Dalrymple reports, 'terrified by the prospect of future alarms, many of the adherents of James quitted the Convention and retired to the country; more of them changed sides; only a very few of the most resolute continued their attendance.'

'The Convention ordered Major Buntin... to go after him'

But without success. Whether it be true that the Major 'never came within sight' of the fugitive, or that he was scared off by a threat of being sent back to his masters 'in a pair of Blanketts', the result of his mission was the same.

6. 'UPON THE FACE OF CAERKETTON'

'Lilliburlero... Newcastle'

Lilliburlero was the ***Marseillaise*** of the Glorious Revolution. The tune first appeared in print in 1686 and was soon afterwards set to satirical verses by one Wharton (see Notes for Chapter 1), playing a part in the discomfiture and self-exile of James II. The tune has been credited to Purcell (it appears in his ***Musick's Handmaid***) although it is possible he 'borrowed' a popular tune of the day. The tune ***Newcastle*** appeared in Playford's famous ***Dancing Master*** published during the Protectorate; it would have been familiar to almost everyone in the late seventeenth century, and is still sometimes heard today.

'Rullion-Green... General Thomas Dalyell'

Soon after the Restoration of 1660, the Episcopal form of

worship was imposed on a largely hostile Scotland. Unofficial Conventicles however were held in the open air by Presbyterian ministers who had resigned or been expelled from their livings. These field-meetings gained great popular support in the South-west which remained the heartland of the Covenanting movement. The government countered by imposing fines for non-attendance at the parish-churches; in 1666, violence by soldiers towards an old man who had not paid his fines, provoked a rebellion by Covenanters in Dumfries. Hoping to gain support en route, they marched towards Edinburgh, but becoming disheartened by failure to attract followers, they turned back at Colinton, a few miles short of their goal. They were intercepted and easily defeated at Rullion Green in the Pentlands by General Thomas Dalziell – a wild character who had served in Russia and refused to cut his beard since the death of Charles I. (The founder of the Scots Greys, his boots – like Dundee reputedly proof against lead bullets, are preserved in The Binns, home of the present Tam Dalziell. He is marvellously portrayed by Scott in the novel ***Old Mortality***.) The prisoners were severely dealt with, some being hanged in the Grassmarket in Edinburgh, others at Glasgow, Irvine, Ayr and Dumfries. The incident inspired R.L.Stevenson to write ***The Pentland Rising*** – his first published work (at sixteen!). The following year (1867) his father took a lease of Swanston Cottage where the young Stevenson was to spend many a happy summer.

'Agag... walk'd upon eggs'

A literal paraphrase of 'Agag came... delicately' (I Sam. 15, 32).

'the Seal'd Knot'

This was a clandestine body of Royalists committed to the restoration of Charles II during the Interregnum. On the death of Cromwell in 1658, they planned a coup – which in the event proved unnecessary; without the Protector's strong hand to guide it, the Commonwealth began to disintegrate forcing General Monck eventually to begin moves leading to the Restoration.

'totally alien in culture, social organization, language'

The Gaelic-speaking clan society of the Highlands, based on personal allegiance to a Chief through (largely imaginary) ties of blood, is an extraordinary example of a 'Shame and Honour' Iron-Age-type warrior society surviving into modern times. Unfortunately, the reaction it provoked among 'civilized' communities was similar to that generated by Red Indians or Australian Aboriginals among nineteenth-century white pioneers. (Yet the moral and social values of these 'savages' were exemplary. Following Culloden, any clansman could have earned a fortune beyond his dreams by betraying the Prince who had ensured the destruction of his society; yet for months the Royal fugitive wandered among the clans in perfect security that his identity would not be revealed. Can the 'Enterprise Culture' show anything to match this?) Actually, the English-speaking Lowlander was more akin in blood to his Highland fellow-Scot than he probably realised – the ethnic composition of both peoples being largely Celtic.

'the equivalent of the grass skirt'

The kilt as worn at the time of Aphra Behn was the 'philamor' or belted plaid, gathered round the waist by a belt from which it hung in pleats at the back, the loose end being thrown over the shoulder and fastened with a pin or brooch. A good representation of the garment can be seen in the portrait of a Highland chief c.1660 in the National Portrait Gallery in Edinburgh. The 'little kilt' or 'philabeg' as worn today did not make its appearance until the 1720's and was, ***horresco referens*** (to quote Aphra Behn's use of a Latin tag), the invention of an Englishman! – one Rawlinson, a Lancashire ironmaster settled in Glengarry, who devised it for the convenience of his workers.

P.S. That every clan had its own tartan is an attractive idea but probably has little foundation in fact. 'Clan' tartans seem largely to have been designed by enterprising manufacturers after the lifting of the ban on Highland Dress in 1782.

7. 'IN PLAIN SIGHT OF THE GRAMPIAN MOUNTAINS'

'The Cat i' the Fable which walk'd in Boots'

The reference a few lines later to the Ogre changing himself into a lion then into a mouse, confirms that the fable is the familiar 'Puss-in-Boots'. There is an apparent anomaly however; I have traced the appearance of the fable to the collection of tales by Charles Perrault, ***Contes de la Mere Oye***, published in 1697 – i.e. eight years after its mention by Aphra Behn! Perhaps Aphra Behn (who was a translator of wide experience and who corresponded with Continental savants and authors) could have seen an early draft of the story? Or Perrault may have borrowed the elements of the tale from an earlier source, known to Aphra Behn.

'sunk in the full perfection of Decaye'

The phrase has about it a ring of Rochester, whom Aphra Behn knew and whose work she passionately admired. It is perhaps a misquotation or an adaptation of his phrase 'The last Perfection of Misery' (***The Discovery***).

'these Horrible Mountains'

In 1689 (and for most of the following century) Highland scenery was regarded with a mixture of distaste and apprehension. 'Frightful', 'horrid', 'desert' are the common coin of travellers' descriptions of the landscape of the Highlands prior to c.1780. Man's mastery of his environment was then too recent and too precarious to allow, in general, of any but a hostile view of Nature Untam'd. However, beginning perhaps with Pope's fascination with grottoes and James Thomson's remarkable poem, ***The Seasons***, a slow reaction against too-regulated landscapes sets in before the middle of the eighteenth century, gathers force with the Ossian Industry created by James MacPherson, and is in full flood by the end of century with the Romantic poets and the young Walter Scott's burgeoning vision – which was soon to release a flood of literary tourists into the Trossachs, copies of ***Rob Roy*** in hand.

8. 'BEYOND THE EDGE'

'Here the stream plunges over a steep Precipice'

From Aphra Behn's description of the place, I think it is probably the Falls of Braan, where the present Rumbling Bridge spans the river above the first of a spectacular series of falls. The other possible candidate is the Hermitage Falls (visible from the charming eighteenth-century summer house 'Ossian's Hall') on the same river, nearer Dunkeld; the Rumbling Bridge site however, matches Aphra Behn's description far more closely.

'the meeting of Bran and a lesser stream'

From topographical descriptions, distances and directions of route mentioned in the Journal, it seems likely that this is the Cochill Burn, through whose glen General Wade was later to drive one of his roads.

'a considerable brook flowing into Lyon from the north'

The only 'brook' that fits this description is the Keltney Burn – quite a formidable river to wade across!

'Sir Thos. Urqhart... Wm. Drummond of Hawthornden'

Sir Thomas Urquart of Cromarty was a flamboyant scholar whose riotous translation of the first book of Rabelais was published in 1653 – during the darkest night of the Puritan repression! William Drummond of Hawthornden (1585 – 1649) wrote elegant poems in English – as opposed to Scots, which can stand comparison with the English metaphysical poets.

'to see a great Marvell and to hear of a greater'

Fortingall today is a prettified village, whose incongruously thatched roofs give it the appearance of having been transplanted from Sussex. Both the yew tree (reputedly 3000 years old) and the amazing story that Fortingall was the birthplace of Pontius Pilate, continue to flourish.

9. 'A BLEAK AND GHASTLIE WILDERNESSE'

'press'd on through a heatherie Valley'

Presumably the valley of the Keltney Burn. (See Notes to Chapter 8.) This would seem to be confirmed later when Aphra Behn says, 'the stream began to trend to the westwards' – which the Keltney Burn does in its upper reaches, where it changes its name to Allt Mor.

'Sir John Campbell'

Known as 'Ian Glas' – Grey John, 'cunning as a fox, wise as a serpent, slippery as an eel', he was one of the principal plotters behind the Glencoe Massacre of 1692. The Massacre itself was carried out by Argyll soldiers under the command of Robert Campbell of Glenlyon.

'Argyll... whose Chief stands high in William's favour'

This was Archibald, 10th Earl, who returned with William of Orange and was made by William 1st Duke. He was the successor to the Archibald who was executed after his ill-fated Rebellion. (See Notes to Chapter 3.)

'MacDonalds... of Glencoe'

Alastair MacDonald of Glencoe (later to be murdered in the Massacre), answered Dundee's call, with a hundred of his sept.

'he had slain the last Wolf in Scotland'

There is some doubt as to the validity of this claim, made in 1680. Slayings of 'last wolves' continued to be reported occasionally – up to 1743, when a hunter named MacQueen was credited with killing the very last Scottish wolf.

'Not so much resembling a Sugar-loaf as I had suppos'd... here the Mountain extends itself in a vast Promontorie'

The 'vast Promontorie' sounds like the spur which forms the eastern flank of Schiehallion, ending in the heathery slopes known as Aonach Ban. From this approach, the mountain takes on its true appearance of a broad-backed ridge. The famous conical profile can be seen to advantage (as Aphra Behn records) from the north side of Loch Rannoch.

'a dreary Desert of low broken ground and beyond it the Mouth of a Monstrous Valley'

Probably Rannoch Moor and the entrance to Glencoe; the description certainly fits.

'a mighty Forest, cov'ring all the sides of the Mountains'

This can only be the Black Wood of Rannoch – more extensive then than now. It is a surviving fragment of the Old Caledonian Forest which once covered much of Scotland.

'a broken hollow Land'

The peat-hagged desolation traversed by the railway connecting Rannoch and Corrour Stations, must surely qualify as one of the bleakest and most remote areas in Britain.

'the Head of a Loch, all hemm'd in with steep high Slopes'

This description fits the appearance of Loch Treig, confirming that the sources which name it as the site of Dundee's last bivouac of his journey to Glen Roy, are correct.

'a Monstrous Wall... one Vast and Horrid Top'

Depending on exactly where Aphra Behn was standing when she saw this view, it could refer to the massif of peaks around the 4000 foot level dominated by Ben Nevis (4406 feet), at the north-western end of Glen Nevis seen from the east. It is certainly tempting to identify the 'Vast and Horrid Top' with Ben Nevis; however, the description could equally apply to the long file of the 'Grey Corries', with its 'Pico or Master-hill' Stob Choire Claurigh, looming above the other tops, at just under 4000 feet.

'I am come to the Summit of the Pass'

The Pass is almost certainly the Lairig Leacach, which provides the only direct access on foot between Loch Treig and Glen Spean.

10. 'I RESOLV'D I WOU'D STEAL INTO DUNDEE'S CAMP'

'there is here a fine Road'

This must be one of the famous 'Parallel Roads' to be found on either side of Glen Spean, and elsewhere. These former shorelines of ice-dammed lakes were at one time known as 'King's Hunting Roads' for it was believed they were man-made.

'a deep and exeeding narrow Gorge'

This sounds very like the Gorge of Achluachrach. Here, before being tapped in 1928 to provide power for the Lochaber Aluminium Works, the Spean was a wild rushing torrent; now however it is much attenuated. A vivid account of the Spean's pre-1928 appearance in the Gorge is provided in ***Mountain, Moor and Loch*** (1895) produced by the North British Railway Company.

'a verie tall man with Moustachios'

This corresponds with contemporary descriptions of Sir Ewen Cameron of Lochiel, who met Dundee on his arrival in Glen Spean and offered him the use of a house near his own. (Lochiel lived at Achnacarry House between Loch Arkaig and Loch Lochy; during the Second World War, Lochiel's descendant was dispossessed of Achnacarry* which became the headquarters for Commando training.) Although probably using the house assigned to him for ceremonial receptions, Dundee lived with his men in their camp at Glen Roy.

'this Intelligence I've learn'd of'

For details of the Strath Spey Campaign, see Appendix: John Graham of Claverhouse.

* A re-building on the site of the original wooden structure that was burned down by Cumberland's troops after Culloden.

11. 'INTELLIGENCE FROM BADENOCH'

'the Generall Support of the People'

This was certainly the case in the South of Scotland, where the vast majority of the people were Presbyterian. Here, William was welcomed as a Liberator from an alien Episcopalian form of worship imposed by a tyrannical Government. The fact that the success of James' cause in Scotland depended on (largely Catholic or Episcopalian) Highland troops, probably reinforced William's popularity in the South of Scotland, where memories of the 'Highland Host' were recent and bitter. (The forced billeting of 5000-8000 Highlanders by Lauderdale on the Covenanting South-west in 1678 in an attempt to crush popular resistance was never forgotten in the Lowlands – nor forgiven.) Beginning with Glencoe, a terrible vengeance was gradually to be wreaked, which amounted to nothing less than the ultimate destruction of Gaeldom. A parallel would be the extirpation of the Red Indian by white pioneers in nineteenth century America.

'a Thing infinitely to be regretted'

Since at least the time of Roger Ascham (who in his ***Toxophilus*** of 1545 ardently championed Anglo-Scottish Union), mainstream thought among leading figures in England and Scotland (two honourable exceptions being Fletcher of Saltoun and Hamilton of Biel) tended to subscribe to the 'Mutual Benefits of Union' theory of which the Incorporating Union of 1707 was seen to be a natural and logical development. Opposition to Union among the ordinary people of Scotland was however always much more widespread, stemming perhaps from a 'gut feeling' that Union constituted a threat to National identity.

'Intelligence which Samuel hath brought me from Badenoch'

Seen in the light of Samuel's spying mission in Badenoch, some of the anomalies of the Strath Spey Campaign are cleared up at a stroke. How did Forbes and MacKay come to be forewarned of Dundee's approach? From where did MacKay get the information regarding Dundee's movements, which enabled him to keep ahead of and finally escape from Dundee, in the breathtaking chase down Strath Spey? Why did MacKay unaccountably turn back when he had Dundee at his mercy? The answers to these questions can be found in Aphra Behn's account in her Journal, of Samuel's report.

12. 'A DESP'RATE PASS'

'his Repute and Standing are assur'd among the Highlanders'

Having expended the best years of his life coping with (to considerable effect) the rigid fanatics of Galloway, Dundee was faced with the task of forging an army from fluid and touchy Highlanders to whom discipline was an alien concept, and acceptance by whom depended on a heroic combination of: charm, tact, patience, sympathy, firmness combined with flexibility, and readiness to live as one of them. That Dundee, a Lowlander, should have succeeded in this daunting task is remarkable. The only other non-Highlanders to have had any success in the same field, are Montrose (a Graham like Dundee), and Prince Charles Edward Stewart, whose fatal charm and military incompetence brought about the demise of the Clan System he exploited for his dynasty's ends.

'urging that he consider wherein his true Dutie lieth'

The Tug of War between Dundee and Murray was to explode into a crisis which caused the Highland Campaign to accelerate swiftly into its final phase. (See Chapters 13 and 14 and their Notes.)

13. 'MADAM WILL YOU TALK?'

'we halted at a straggling Clachan'

This (as is confirmed in Chapter 14) was Struan. From her topographical references, it sounds as though Aphra Behn reached it via Loch Laggan, the Pass of Drumochter and Glen Garry – the route most tourists today would take.

'Madam will you talk?'

The song features in M.R. James' ghost story ***Martin's Close***, the action of which takes place in 1683, as a new West Country ditty.

'Major Snell, one of Kirke's Lambs'

I have been unable to trace this officer in Army Records, which is however no reason to suppose he was not speaking the truth; there are no muster rolls extant for the time of Sedgemoor (6th July 1685), and the annual pay rolls vary enormously. (These can be studied in the Public Record Office – War Office Class 24/7&8 and 25/3206.)

'Dr. Mews was shifting the Cannon to the Centre'

Dr. Mews was the militant Bishop of Winchester who personally supervised the repositioning and firing of the Royalist Artillery at Sedgemoor. Kirke's regiment was switched from the left to the right of the Royalist line during these manoeuvres which accords with Snell's account of the cause of his injuries.

'Melfort, I fear, is a Bungling Fool'

John Drummond, Duke of Melfort, was James II's Chief Advisor and also his ***Bête Noire***: he helped to ruin James' popularity as a King, he ruined his cause in the Convention (see Chapter 4), he totally mismanaged the commissariat for the troops besieging Londonderry, and he kept Dundee in Scotland starved of supplies.

'the Boot'

A Scottish instrument of torture. It consisted of an iron frame enclosing the leg. Wedges were then driven between it and the limb which was crushed in consequence.

'the Reports concerning Bloodie Claverhouse'

Defoe, Wodrow, Walker and other apologists for the Covenanters seem to have uncritically accepted the anti-Claverhouse propaganda generated by the Conventiclers and their sympathisers, and by including this propaganda in their published works have helped to perpetuate the myth of 'Bloody Clavers'. In many cases where records survive*, Claverhouse can be shown to have acted justly, and in the main mercifully, when dealing with the Covenanters. One example may suffice by way of illustration. John Brownen, an armed rebel, was captured by Claverhouse and handed over to the Lieutenant-General. Claverhouse then wrote a long letter to the Earl of Queensberry pleading for mercy for Brownen who 'has been but a month or two with his halbert'.

'I wade across the Ford... splash thorough a little Tributarie'

Today, there is a ford across the Garry about a mile to the east of Struan. This ford is just above where a 'little Tributarie', the Bruar, enters the Garry, so it may well be the one that Aphra Behn used. (A little upstream of its confluence with the Garry, the Bruar has some spectacular falls, the subject of a well-known poem by Robert Burns.)

'a Mightie Keep'

This is Blair Castle – shorn of its eighteenth and nineteenth century accretions. The 'Tug of War' between Dundee and Lord John Murray (see Notes to Chapter 12) was approaching a climax when Aphra Behn arrived on the scene.

* The Queensberry Papers are especially important in this context.

14. 'KILLY-CRANKIE'

'Stewart of Ballechin... hath seiz'd the Castle for King James'

The final moves in the Game for Three Players (Dundee, MacKay and Murray) in the run-up to Killiecrankie, were swift and complex. Shortage of Provisions in Lochaber forced Dundee to leave his base there at times; it was from temporary headquarters at Struan (only two and a half miles from Blair on the other side of the Garry) that Dundee launched his mid-July letter campaign against Murray, urging him to come over to King James. Receiving no reply, Dundee ordered Murray's Steward, Stewart of Ballechin, to take the Castle for King James – a task which that enthusiastic Jacobite was delighted to perform, forcing Murray to besiege his own home. Still Dundee persevered with Murray (who was also being bombarded with missives from his master, MacKay); moving to Badenoch in the third week of July, Dundee made two final written appeals to Murray from Garva on the Spey shortly after arriving there on the 23rd. The bearers of the letter returned to Badenoch with the news that not only would Murray not see them, but that MacKay was at Perth ***en route*** to occupy Blair Castle. On the 26th Dundee marched to Blair, MacKay marched to Dunkeld, the clansmen of Murray's besieging force led by the young Simon Fraser of Lovat, mutinied and went over to Dundee, and Murray, abandoning Blair, retreated to Moulin by Pitlochry, via the Pass of Killiecrankie. (See Appendix: John Graham of Claverhouse.)

'the Fusileers, Edinburgh and Hasting's Regiment'

Regiments were then usually named after their Commanding Officers, but could be otherwise designated. Thus, Buchan's Regiment was also the Royal Scots Fusiliers (in which Sir Ewen Cameron of Lochiel's son served). Leven's Regiment was also the Edinburgh Regiment (raised in 1689 for the defence of the City during the siege of the Castle), later re-named The King's Own Scottish Borderers, as a result of a squabble with the Lord Provost; on March 18th 1989 the Regiment celebrated its tercentenary, exercising its ancient right to march through the City with drums beating, colours flying and bayonets fixed. Hasting's Regiment (MacKay's sole English contingent) was also known as Leslie's Regiment after its Colonel.

'a Trooper cries out... and sways in the Saddle, then he falls'

According to tradition, the sniper was an intrepid Highland marksman and scout Ian Beg MacRae, who, by a single shot fired across the Garry, brought his victim down near a spring subsequently called 'Fuaran u Trupar' – 'Well of the Trooper'.

'a Highland Armie a-coming down the Hillside upon us!'

A study of the relevant Ordnance Survey Map (Sheet 48 in the old 'One Inch' Series) is a help in appreciating Dundee's successful ruse. MacKay expected Dundee to advance along the Garry directly from Blair; the 'small Parties of the Enemie' approaching from the expected direction, completely fooled MacKay (who viewed them from the rising ground around Aldclune) into thinking they were the advance guard of Dundee's army. Meanwhile, Dundee had taken his army across the Tilt, come over the hill by Lude, and was dropping down to the hollow of the Clune Burn when MacKay finally became aware of what was happening. Galloping back to his troops, MacKay, in a desperate bid to occupy the high ground before Dundee, marched his army up through the woods of Urrard onto what proved to be a 'False Summit' – to find Dundee's army waiting for him on the real summit above him.

'struggle to fix their Bayonetts in the Muzzles of their Firelocks'

Combining the pike and firearm into a single weapon could prove to be a disastrous liability when the two became mutually exclusive – as happened at Killiecrankie. MacKay, who survived the battle, learned from the experience and scrapped the plug bayonet (first issued to British troops in 1672), instituting the present system where the bayonet is clipped to the outside of the muzzle.

'Charging my Piece with one of Sir Isaac's... Silvern Bullets'

The legend that Claverhouse was proof against lead bullets has already been mentioned in the Notes to Chapter 2. An extension of this legend is the tradition (mentioned by Scott in his Notes to ***Old Mortality***, and by other writers) that Claverhouse was killed by a silver bullet. In this instance it would seem that tradition and fact are interconnected.

'a Broken Waste of Hills and Mosses'

An apt description of the country between the Upper Tummel and the Upper Tay which the fugitives would have crossed on their flight to Weem.

'seek Refuge in Castle Mingis'

An impressive pile, Castle Menzies is today a clan museum. It was MacKay's first stop on his headlong flight from the battlefield, ***en route*** to Stirling.

APPENDIX

SUMMARIES OF THE LIVES OF APHRA BEHN, GILBERT BURNET AND VISCOUNT DUNDEE.

Aphra Behn

1640 Born in Kent to Bartholomew and Elizabeth Johnson.

1663 Sails to Surinam (then British) in South America with her father (who dies on voyage).

1664 Returns to England. Marries Mr. Behn, a merchant 'of Dutch extraction'.

1666 Widowed. Engages attention of Charles II by her wit; sent by him to Antwerp as a spy, in the Anglo-Dutch War. Sends Report to government re. Dutch plans to send fleet to attack Thames-Medway estuary. (Her Report was ignored!)

1668 Imprisoned for debt following her return from Flanders. (Government dragging its feet over paying her expenses as spy.) On her release, decides to support herself by writing – an amazing stance for a woman in the 17th century!

1670 – 1678 Series of plays, mostly very successful – *The Forc'd Marriage, The Amorous Prince, The Rover* (inspired by her tragic affair with atheist and bisexual lawyer John Hoyle), the latter a box-office triumph which earned her the patronage of Duke of York, the future James II. Campaigns vigorously for 'Equal Rights for Women' – not just as writers, but concerning their place in society.

1678 – 1681 A comparative break from the Theatre. Deeply affected by Hoyle's desertion of her, and by death of the wit and poet Rochester whom she passionately admired. Loyally supports her patron Duke of York in poems and pamphlets, at a time when the Popish Plot and Monmouth's propaganda campaign have made the future monarch deeply unpopular. Censured by Gilbert Burnet (see below) for the frank eroticism of her writings.

1681 – 1687 Fortunes vary as plays – *The Roundheads, The City Heiress, The Emperor of the Moon* (revived in Edinburgh some years ago), etc. were successful or otherwise. A poem praising Creech's translation of Lucretius' opus pioneering the Atomic Theory and Determinism, a novella *Love Letters, Part I,* political verse, and a collection of her poems *A Voyage to the Island of Love* also produced. *Ode on the Coronation of James II* was perhaps her finest work at this period. Her circle – Otway, Buckingham, Waller (and soon Nell Gwynne) begin to die off. Her energy, health and financial position deteriorate.

1688 A daring Introductory Essay to her translation of Fontenelle's *Discovery of New Worlds*, in which she: defies St.Paul's maxim about women preaching, demands that the new sciences be as accessible to women as to men, develops a theory of comparative philology, constructs a spirited argument defending the Copernican Theory, and corrects an error regarding the height of the earth's atmosphere – more than enough to establish for her the reputation of a savante!

June: Publication of her novel *Oroonoko* (featuring a black hero, and drawing on her memories of Surinam for its setting) – regarded by some as her masterpiece, remarkable for its stance on racial equality, and probably influenced the development of Anti-Slavery movement.

N.B. *Oroonoko* is dedicated to Richard Maitland of the celebrated East Lothian family of that name. (Seat, until the death of John Maitland Duke of Lauderdale in 1682 – Lethington Tower, now known as Lennoxglove, near Haddington. Monument in Lauderdale Aisle in St. Mary's Haddington, adjoining family vault; Richard Maitland recorded on memorial tablet.) An interesting example of the 'East Lothian Connection'. (See below.)

October: Falls passionately (but unrequitedly) in love with Hortense Mancini – an Italian adventuress, to whom she dedicates *The History of the Nun*.

November – December. Prostrated by general abandonment

of her old patron James II, following landing of William of Orange. (Her sentiments apparent in the Dedication of her story *The Lucky Mistake*.)

1689 February: *Congratulatory Poem to Queen Mary* (whom, as James II's daughter she was prepared to accept; the total absence of any reference in the poem to William, is telling).

March: Sinking fast. Visited by Gilbert Burnet who probably tries to persuade her to write a pindaric celebrating William of Orange's achievements, for the forthcoming coronation. Instead, she writes *A Pindaric Poem to the Reverend Dr. Burnet (for) enquiring after me and my Muse*. (Published in broadsheet and considered one of her best poems; in it she re-affirms her recognition of Mary's right to succeed to the throne, but not William's.)

April 16th: Dies.

April 20th: Buried in Westminster Abbey.

N.B. The events of her life for 1689, from March, now of course have to be re-interpreted in the light of her Journal.

Gilbert Burnet

1643 Born in Edinburgh. Father an advocate of good Aberdeen Family.

1653 Enters Marischal College Aberdeen. Studies Law and Divinity. M.A. at sixteen.

1663 – 1664 Visits Cambridge, Oxford, London, Holland (where he rubs shoulders with numerous religious sects, and studies Hebrew).

1669 Appointed Professor of Divinity at Glasgow University, resigns because of Lauderdale's enmity. Moves to London where appointed Chaplain of Rolls Chapel (extremely popular preacher) and Lecturer at St. Clements.

1679 Publication of Parts I and II of his *History of the Reformation in England*, also, *Some Passages in the Life and Death of the Earl of Rochester*. Resists Royal pressure to break with liberal moderates, and in consequence deprived of Lectureship by Charles II.

1684 Preaches vehement anti-Papal sermon (to great applause) which angers Duke of York (soon to succeed as James II).

1685 – 1688 On James' accession flees to Continent to avoid Royal vengeance. Buttonholes and lectures Louis XIV! Tours southern France – writes to William of Orange *et al* deploring persecution of Huguenots. Joins William of Orange in Holland, becomes a favourite and William's chief 'P.R. man'.

1688 November: Accompanies William as Royal chaplain on board the invasion fleet bound for England. Draws up William's Declaration of Intent and has it read in Exeter. Appointed in charge of good behaviour of William's troops towards civilians *en route* to London. Acts as go-between on behalf of William, and John Graham of Claverhouse – Viscount Dundee as of 12th November. (Claverhouse, who had accompanied the army in Scotland south to support James, remains loyal to him amid general desertion – including John Churchill later Duke of Marlborough, to William. William wishes to discover Claverhouse's intentions, and invites him to enter his service. Claverhouse refuses, and later returns to Scotland – in February of the New Year.)

December: Arranges 'escape' of James to France. Secures protection for Catholics and supporters of James in London.

1689 January: Delivers Thanksgiving Sermon on the triumph of the Glorious Revolution at St. James.

March: Visits Aphra Behn (see above.) Consecrated Bishop of Salisbury.

April 11th: Preaches sermon at joint Coronation of William and Mary.

N.B. I have broken off here, as Aphra Behn 'dies' five days after the Cornonation.

P.S. The 'East Lothian Connection'. That Aphra Behn, who spent most of her life in London and the Home Counties, should have had close (if fortuitous) links with East Lothian, seems on the face of it unlikely. But by a quirk of fate, she was destined to have dealings, directly or indirectly, with gentlemen from 'Haddingtonshire' – Richard Maitland, Gilbert Burnet, Burnet's old pupil Fletcher of Saltoun, Hamilton of Biel, etc.

John Graham of Claverhouse, Viscount Dundee

1648 – 1672 Born to William Graham of Claverhouse and Lady Magdalene Carnegie. M.A. at St.Andrews University. Justice of Peace for Forfarshire.

1672 – 1678 Serves abroad, first in French army (together with John Churchill later Duke of Marlborough), then (along with Hugh MacKay his future opponent at Killiecrankie), under William of Orange as a Cornet in his personal guard. Credited with saving William's life at Battle of Seneff. Returns to Scotland, perhaps because of disappointment concerning promotion.

1678 – 1679 Captain of Dragoons in Royal Horse Guards, sent to Galloway to suppress illegal 'field-meetings' or Conventicles, of Covenanters (extreme Presbyterians who refused to accept Established Episcopal form of worship). Appointed Sherriff-depute of Dumfriesshire and Wigtonshire to give him legal backing for his task. Covenanter Rebellion breaks out following Murder of Archbishop Sharp. (See Notes for Chapter 4.) Claverhouse surprises large armed band of Covenanters and is defeated by them at skirmish of Drumclog. Rebellion crushed at Bothwell Brig by Duke of Monmouth. (Claverhouse present at battle.)

1679 – 1682 Records scanty. Judicial circuit in Galloway in aftermath of Bothwell Brig. Stays in London.

1682 – 1684 Appointed heritable Sherriff of Wigton with task of suppressing Conventicles in Galloway. 'Pacification' of region achieved by firm but impartial imposition of the law. Marries Jean Cochrane (from family of notorious Covenanting ties and sympathies!)

1684 – 1685. Carries out rigorous measures against Covenanters (always within the law, however), following fanatical Renwick's Declaration against the government; the so-called 'Killing-Time'. Apologists for Covenanters (Wodrow, Defoe, etc.) later accuse Claverhouse of carrying out many summary executions at this time, but without conclusive evidence.

1685 – 1688 Records scanty. Promoted to Major-General. Appointed Provost of Dundee.

1688 Accompanies army in Scotland south to help James, in face of invasion threat from William of Orange. Remains loyal to James when most leaders desert to William. Meets Gilbert Burnet who passes on message from William appealing (unsuccessfully) to Claverhouse (now Viscount Dundee) to join him.

1689 February: Returns to Scotland.

March: Persuades Duke of Gordon to continue holding Edinburgh Castle for James. Attends the Convention, but following the Convention's decision to choose William as King, returns to Dudhope, his home near Dundee. Declared a traitor by the Convention.

April: Dundee's Commission (appointing him Lieutenant-General and Commander-in-Chief in Scotland) sent from James in Ireland but falls into hands of the Convention. Nevertheless, Dundee raises Royal Standard and with a small personal following heads north to rally the clans for James. (His success in this due to his appealing to clan Chiefs on a personal level, by meetings and letters. By contrast, MacKay's attempts to win over the clans were flat-footed and inept – and unsuccessful, despite MacKay being a Highlander born and bred, whereas Dundee was a Lowlander!) Detours south again to await hoped-for reinforcements from Ireland and deserters from old fellow-soldiers in Williamite army in Dundee. However, hearing of approach of the Williamite Commander-in-Chief General MacKay (his old fellow-campaigner), he falls back to Castle Gordon. Disappointed of help promised by Keppoch (an irresponsible freebooter), Dundee was forced to retreat to Badenoch, leaving Elgin and Inverness to be occupied by MacKay.

6th or 7th May: Issues letters to clans to meet him in Lochaber on the 18th.

10th May: Lightning raid from Badenoch, on Dunkeld (via Blair) where he 'liberates' revenues collected by Williamite Officers. Pushes on to Perth (the same night!) and annexes military supplies.

13th May: Appears before town of Dundee (having marched via Scone collecting revenues and volunteers) hoping to be joined by deserters mentioned above. They fail to break out so Dundee falls back on nearby Glen Ogilvy, his old home.

14th May: Sets out for Lochaber to keep appointment with the clans.

16th May: Arrives at rendezvous in Lochaber after heroic forced march via Rannoch, Loch Treig and eastern flank of Ben Nevis. (Choice of route determined by need to avoid MacKay's forces. To have covered the distance in two days, during a bitterly cold late spring, is an incredible achievement, as a glance at a map will show.) Received by venerated clan Chief, Cameron of Lochiel, whose influence crucial to gaining support of clans. The Fiery Cross sent round.

25th May: Review of clans. Highland army sets out for Strath Spey.

29th May: Castle Ruthven near Kingussie surrenders to Dundee.

1st-4th June: Dundee chases MacKay down Strath Spey but just fails to catch him before MacKay links up with reinforcements on flat terrain unsuitable for Highland mode of battle. (By this time Dundee has earned *the clansmen's loyalty and respect* – a vital factor, by sharing their privations and getting to know them personally.)

6th June: Dundee begins retreat back down Strath Spey for Badenoch pursued by a now heavily reinforced MacKay. Dundee now ill.

10th June: Dundee arrives back in Lochaber. Yielding to necessity, he dismisses Highland army so that they can take their booty home, with injunctions to be ready to assemble again soon. Inexplicably, MacKay heads back for Inverness (and eventually to Edinburgh). Score so far: nil – nil.

Mid-June to mid-July: A lull in the campaign. Dundee uses interval to train up newly-arrived MacLeans, and consolidate his status with the clan Chiefs by a flow of personal letters. His Commission from King James finally arrives, enhancing his authority. Clans commanded to assemble at Blair Atholl on 29th July. (Blair Castle, situated between Passes of Drumochter and Killiecrankie, of vital strategic importance.)

Late July: 16th-26th: A crisis. Lord John Murray – Marquis of Atholl's eldest son, arrives in Highlands to try (on MacKay's instructions) to prevent the men of Atholl from siding with Dundee. Dundee counters, by persuading Murray's factor to seize Blair Castle (the Murray family Seat!) and hold it for King James.

26th July: Atholl clansmen, on discovering Murray's intentions, reject him and declare for Dundee. Murray abandons Blair and falls back to Moulin near Pitlochry. Dundee arrives at Blair, via Pass of Drumochter. MacKay (aware of Blair's strategic importance) marches from Perth to Dunkeld; learning of Murray's retreat, he sends Colonel Lauder to hold the Pass of Killiecrankie open so that the army can reach Blair.

27th July, dawn: Dundee holds council of war to decide whether to wait for rest of clans or to confront MacKay. (As all the clans have not yet assembled, he has only 2000 men compared to MacKay's 4000-plus.) MacKay marches north for Blair.

10 a.m.: MacKay arrives at southern end of Pass of Killiecrankie.

Noon: MacKay begins threading the Pass. Dundee moves to deploy clans on high ground above northern entry to Pass.

Late afternoon: MacKay emerges from Pass, wheels his army round in extended formation to face Dundee above him. MacKay thus has rising ground in front of him, a steep slope down to the River Garry behind him, and his army strung out in a long line – the worst possible conditions in which to meet a Highland charge!

Early evening: Armies confront each other while sun goes down. (Dundee intends to postpone attack until sun no longer in his men's eyes.)

8 p.m.: Sun dips behind mountains. Highland army charges – MacKay's forces annihilated in two minutes. (Dundee struck by a bullet below the armpit as he waves on his men; dies shortly after. MacKay 'softly' joins flight and manages to escape to Weem.)

P.S. Lacking Dundee's leadership, the morale of the Highland army crumbles; soon after Killiecrankie it is defeated – first at Dunkeld, then conclusively at Cromdale, and (for the time being) the Jacobite Cause is lost.

The maps are extracts from Herman Moll's Map of Scotland of 1714. Despite some omissions and errors (e.g. Loch Eggan for Loch Laggan), Moll's map is reasonably accurate and gives a pleasing amount of detail; many of the place-names mentioned by Aphra Behn (especially in Lothian) can be readily picked out.